ONE

D0380175

"It hasn't registered, has it?" ...ed. "It's over. There's nothing between us."

Alex's voice was chillingly even. "You mean you've had your fun, now you just want a quiet life."

He pulled her roughly into a doorway. "Alex, why are you doing this? Can't you understand? I've got a whole life going with someone else. A very happy one."

Her shell of vulnerability cracked, revealing a brittle bitterness. "If your life's so damn complete, what were you doing with me?"

It was like a slap across the face. He felt his anger. "Is this why you had to see me?" Gallagher demanded. "Is that what you want to talk about? Our imaginary love affair?"

"I'm pregnant," she said. . . .

Fatal ATTRACTION

A novel by H.B. Gilmour
based on the screenplay by James Dearden

A SIGNET BOOK

NEW AMERICAN LIBRARY

PUBLISHER'S NOTE

This book is a work of fiction. Names, characters, places, and incidents either are the product of the author's imagination or are used fictitiously, and any resemblance to actual persons, living or dead, events, or locales is entirely coincidental.

NAL BOOKS ARE AVAILABLE AT QUANTITY DISCOUNTS WHEN USED TO PROMOTE PRODUCTS OR SERVICES. FOR INFORMATION PLEASE WRITE TO PREMIUM MARKETING DIVISION, NEW AMERICAN LIBRARY, 1633 BROADWAY, NEW YORK, NEW YORK 10019.

SIGNET TRADEMARK REG. U.S. PAT. OFF. AND FOREIGN COUNTRIES
REGISTERED TRADEMARK—MARCA REGISTRADA
HECHO EN CHICAGO, U.S.A.

SIGNET, SIGNET CLASSIC, MENTOR, ONYX, PLUME, MERIDIAN and NAL BOOKS are published by NAL PENGUIN INC., 1633 Broadway, New York, New York 10019

First Printing, April, 1988

1 2 3 4 5 6 7 8 9

PRINTED IN THE UNITED STATES OF AMERICA

— 1 —

Dan Gallagher set down the yellow legal pad he was flipping through and glanced up over the rim of his reading glasses. Schubert's Symphony No. 4 poured through the earphones clamped to his head, flooding him with a sense of unshakable contentment.

Maybe it was the music that influenced what he saw, but the rambling old West Side apartment that he and Beth had conquered, room by room, year by year, looked perfect to him tonight. The oak moldings and door frames they'd discovered under layers of grease and paint glowed proudly. The walls they'd scraped and sanded, plastered and papered, were nearly smooth now. Each piece of furniture in the spacious, handsome living room had its own history, its own vintage.

The rolltop desk in the corner was a dinosaur from Dan's law school days. The snazzy new matte-black Italian lamp was Beth's Father's Day bargain from Bloomingdale's last year, when she'd tied a pair of opera tickets to it. Now it craned like an anorexic busybody over the plump shoulder of the easy chair that had been their very first "furniture investment" nine years ago.

And there was Beth, everywhere. Pictures of her were perched on the end table next to the sofa, on the record rack, on the mahogany piano, and the mantel of the fireplace that had never worked—smiling at him with boundless energy, humor, and love.

Beth was there, too, in the amazing brown-eyed gamin curled against a corner of the sofa. Bathed in the silver light of the television screen, the rapt face of Dan's five-year-old daughter, Ellen, made him shake his head and smile.

He had everything he wanted here. Why the hell were they thinking of moving? Why were they going up to Beth's parents' place this weekend to look for a house in Westchester?

Leave well enough alone.

Jesus, Dan thought, where had that come

from? *Leave well enough alone.* It sounded like something his mother would have said.

He waved his hand in front of his daughter's eyes, momentarily blocking her view of the screen. No dice. With a distracted little frown, Ellen moved her head around his hand, oblivious to the attempt at breaking her concentration.

Dan capitulated with a smile, and returned his attention to the Schubert symphony and the law brief in his lap. Then Beth hurried through the room. She tripped over the earphone extension cord, then followed it with her eyes to him, and laughed.

He caught her powdery clean scent as she passed in a blur of trim bare thighs and white cotton bikinis. After more than a decade of watching that velvety muscular body, the sight of his wife still stirred him. Her constantly changing face was built on a bedrock of wonderful bones and a smiling disposition. Sultry or pensive or alive with laughter, her generous lips and crinkly eyes thrilled him. And he loved the screwy thick auburn hair she'd finally stopped trying to control.

God, I'm a lucky bastard, Dan Gallagher thought.

And he was instinctively sorry, instantly apprehensive. Guilty. As if he were some punk who had spray-painted the thought on the wall of a cathedral.

What was it about contentment that made people nervous? Gallagher wondered. What was it that had made him punctuate a moment of pleasure with a shiver of dread?

"Better get going, kiddo," Beth cautioned. "We're going to be late."

"He can't hear you, Mommy," Ellen called after her, without turning from the television set.

The phone rang.

"Oh great," Beth muttered, hesitating. "Dan," she said, then continued into the bathroom.

At the second ring, Ellen glanced from the TV screen to her father and back again. At the third ring, she scrambled to her feet on the sofa, leaned precariously across the armrest, and tugged off one side of his earphones. "Daddy! Telephone!" she hollered.

Startled, it took Dan a moment. "Oh, thanks, honey," he said, standing. His legs were bare. In his crisp white shirt, and tie, shorts, and socks, Dan headed for the phone.

Ellen giggled, then cast a sympathetic glance at Quincy, the Gallaghers' lumbering golden retriever, over whom her father had just tripped. A moment later, when Dan stubbed his toe and grumbled, "Shit!" Ellen shrugged her slender shoulders at the old dog. Then she hopped off the sofa and went into the bathroom to watch her mother put on her makeup.

Grimacing and massaging his foot, Dan answered the phone. It was Hildy calling to find out what Beth was wearing to the book party.

Hildy's husband, James P. Lawrence, Esq. worked with Dan at Miller, Goodman & Hurst. Hildy was pretty and slim, and Jimmy, though at least fifty pounds overweight, was a real plugger. He had a terrific sense of humor and a ready laugh and he was one of those easygoing, big-hearted guys whose presence at the firm made Dan's twelve-hour days seem more like eight.

"Is it going to be 'smart'?" Hildy asked.

"You know what these things are like," Dan reminded her. "It's business."

"Sure, Gallagher," she teased. "Business. Jimmy specialized in family law, remember. I know what to wear to a custody hearing. But you're on the glamorous corporate side of things. I thought I'd better check with Beth about tonight."

Dan laughed. He called questions into Beth and dutifully passed along her replies to Hildy: "She's wearing the black suit. Don't be late . . . she said that, I didn't. Yes, she thinks your red dress is perfect. Okay, see you later. 'Bye, Hildy."

He glanced into the bathroom. Beth's mouth was frothy with toothpaste. She hadn't noticed Ellen playing with her makeup yet.

"Where's my blue suit?" Dan asked her on his way into the bedroom. "Did you pick it up today?"

She mumbled something. Rinsed her mouth. Called to him, "It's on the . . . shit."

"The what?"

"Ellen, please, honey," Beth said. "Don't play with my makeup. Oh, honey, now look."

He craned to see them. Beth was rinsing off Ellen's face, which was streaked with lipstick. Dan smiled. "The suit?"

The doorbell rang. "Oh, no. That must be Christie. What time is it?" Beth straightened up abruptly, knocking a jar of cream to the floor, where it shattered with a splat.

"Shit!" she shouted. "It's on the back door, Dan. Watch out for the glass, honey," she warned Ellen. "Oh, shit, shit, shit. Dan, baby, come in here. My hands are covered with cream. Your suit's on the back of the door. Ellen, honey, let Christie in, okay?"

"Okay," Ellen said cheerfully. In her bare feet and long T-shirt, she waddled down the corridor, singing "Shit, shit shit."

The Japanese restaurant was huge, elegantly black-lacquered, and packed. Robbins and Hart, the publishing house whose legal work Dan did, had taken the place over for the night. They were launching a new book. It looked like they'd pulled out most of the stops for this one.

The floor had been cleared of tables to accommodate the crowd and facilitate the networking flow. There were two open bars downstairs, both mobbed, and another on the balcony, which was bright with the lights of an "Entertainment Tonight" mini-cam crew. That meant, Dan knew, that someone—the book's agent, editor, or author—had connections in the Hollywood/New York TV axis, that someone had invited enough movers and shakers, starlets and newsmakers, to rate a ten-second spot on "ET," or at least a shot at it.

Waitresses in kimonos squeezed through the crowd with trays of hors d'oeuvres—caviar, sushi and sashimi, steamed vegetables, and shrimp tempura. Here and there raised arms, hands gripping drinks, rose above the fray.

Robbins and Hart had set up a little desk at the entrance, where two attractive young publicists—one male, one female, both wearing blond ponytails—were checking invitations against computerized guest lists. Dan handed his invitation to the girl, who hardly glanced at it. She looked past him to Beth. "Oh, God, you're on 'The Young and the Restless,' right? You're Deirdre."

Beth offered one of her most dazzling smiles. "No. I'm afraid not. I'm not an actress."

"Gallagher," Dan said. "Dan and Deirdre—"

"He's kidding." Beth poked him. "Dan and *Beth* Gallagher."

The boy looked over at Beth, too. His eyes swept her from head to toe. "God, I love that suit," he said.

She did look wonderful, Dan thought as they worked their way toward the stairs. Her hair was swept up, held in place by a comb. Her black suit was a knockout, tailored and chic with the jacket on, strapless and sexy without it. Before he could comment on it, one of R&H's house lawyers waved at him.

"Hey, Chuckie," he called to the lanky young man, "you playing ball on Friday? We're in the cellar, can use every lawyer we got. . . ."

A handsomely tanned older man pounded his back.

"Ezra, hey, great to see you," Dan said enthusiastically. "Hi, yeah, I mean, no, next week . . . uh, Wednesday, yeah, see you in court."

Beth squeezed his arm as they moved into the crowd. "God, you look elegant tonight," she told him.

He brushed the back of her neck with his nose.

"Is my hair okay?" She laughed.

"You look great. You smell great. Your hair is great."

"Your nose is cold." She turned and popped an hors d'oeuvre into his mouth.

"Moo know mwhah they say," he said, then swallowed. "Er, you know what they say: 'cold nose, warm—uh-oh!" He spotted Bob Drimmer heading their way.

"Warm uh-oh?" Beth asked.

Dan cleared his throat and assumed the gracious, masklike business smile that told her to cool it. She did, turning with radiant expectation toward the approaching stranger. "Hi, Bob," Dan said. "How's it going?"

Bob Drimmer, senior editor at Robbins and Hart, worked his way toward them. He was wearing a neck brace. His eyes darted from side to side as he pumped Dan's hand. His mind seemed already on the next move.

"Glad you could make it, Dan. Sorry about the meeting tomorrow. I know it's Saturday, but we've got a real crisis."

"That's okay. I've been looking over the pages you sent. Made a few notes. Got a few questions. No problem. This is my wife, Beth. Bob Drimmer."

"How do you do," she said.

His darting eyes settled for a moment on her face, swept down to her cleavage, and back up again. His anxious face relaxed for an instant, flushed with pleasure.

Dan cleared his throat. "There's Hildy."

Beth followed his eyes. Hildy was waving to them over a sea of heads. Beth's face lit up. She waved back.

"I hope you like sushi," Bob said.

"Love it," Dan replied.

Drimmer turned to Beth. "Pleased to meet you," he said, and moved on.

"I believe him," Dan said.

She took his hand and they pushed forward through the crush toward Hildy and Jimmy.

"Who was that?" Jimmy asked. "The guy in the neck brace—"

"Drimmer of Robbins and Hart."

"Your weekend date?" Jimmy laughed.

"What happened to his neck?" Beth asked.

"He was making love to his wife."

She always fell for his stories. "Are you serious?" she whispered. She turned to Hildy, who rolled her eyes. "Oh," Beth said, realizing she'd been had again. "Dan!"

He raised his right hand. "It's the truth."

Jimmy nodded. "You should see his wife— they had to take her away on a stretcher."

"Love hurts," Hildy said dryly.

"Drinks?"

"White wine, please."

Jimmy nodded toward the mob separating them from the bar. "It's a dirty job, Dan," he said, clapping Gallagher on the shoulder, "but someone's got to do it. Get me a vodka on the rocks."

"Come on." They began to make their way toward the bar. It was slow going. One moment Hildy and Beth were with them; the next, they were gone. Dan looked back and saw them laughing together, oblivious to the loss.

A waiter with a tray of drinks slipped through the crush. Jimmy's arm shot out instinctively and seized a champagne. He twirled triumphantly toward Dan, who'd made a pass at the tray but failed to score. But Jimmy's victory was short-lived. He raised his glass only to have his arm jogged by a tweedy type elbowing past. The wine emptied all over his shirtfront.

"Thank you!" Jimmy called out graciously.

Dan laughed and handed over his handkerchief.

"Fuck . . ." Jimmy dabbed ineffectually at the sopping pin-striped shirt. "What great cultural event are we here to celebrate anyway?"

"Some new exercise manual."

Jimmy Lawrence groaned. "Not another one."

"This one's different. It's by some Japanese guy. It's based on ancient Samurai disciplines. Up there," Dan said, pointing to the balcony where the author stood greeting guests in front of a table display of his books.

"What's wrong with him, he keeps nodding and bowing."

"Ancient neck exercise."

"Ahhhhh," said Jimmy, bowing.

They did a couple of minutes of nodding, bowing, and growling, "Saturday Night Live" samurai-style. Finally Dan switched to a little Three Stooges action, and conked Jimmy lightly on the forehead. "Now hand-to-mouth exercise, for which we need drink, yes?"

"*Hai!*" Jimmy bowed again. Then, "Hi, there," he crooned at an extremely attractive blonde passing by. She was wrapped in a metallic black silk outfit that did great things for her body, which actually didn't need a whole lot of help. She had creamy skin and long, jungle-wild hair. Excellent bones. Classy face. Thick black lashes swept up to reveal piercing green eyes—which shot icy daggers at Jimmy. He clutched his chest. "Oh, my God. Death by lethal rejection. If looks could kill . . ."

Dan shook his head. "Very good, Jimmy. I see you haven't lost your touch. Great moves. Very nice."

"Come on, she's hot for me," Jimmy laughed. "Did you see that look? Girl had to tear her eyes away. No pride. I hate a woman who's easy."

They made it to the bar about ten minutes later. After a drink apiece, Jimmy picked up two white wines and set off in search of Beth and Hildy, and Dan started the long, good fight to the men's room. Arthur Ashley, one of the senior partners at Miller, Goodman & Hurst, was standing at a urinal.

"Hi, Arthur."

"That you, Gallagher?"

"Yeah," Dan said, "How's it going?"

Arthur Ashley was an impressive man, easy-going in manner and stately in appearance. Even at a urinal, Dan thought.

"Fine," Arthur said. "You still thinking about moving to the country?"

"We're still talking about it." Dan made it casual. No big deal. Something about Arthur made him cautious. Possibly it was that the man held a mortgage on his future.

"I tried it once—for about four years. Hartsdale."

"Yeah? And?"

Arthur shrugged. "Couldn't take the commute. The trains were always breaking down. What I should have done"—he glanced significantly over his shoulder at Dan—"was waited until they made me a partner."

"Yeah. Well," Dan said. "See you later, Arthur."

Great, he thought, exiting. Now what the hell was that all about? All the way to the bar he tried to figure out the significance of the look. The words. It had sounded almost like Arthur was saying, "I should have waited to become a partner like you've waited, you clever boy." Were they thinking of making him a partner? Relax, Dan told himself. Let it go. Forget stately Arthur and his cryptic small talk.

But it wasn't that easy. He moved up to the bar and ordered a champagne, still distracted by what Arthur seemed to have been hinting at. He was so distracted that he almost bumped into the blonde who had cold-shouldered Jimmy.

She was standing right next to him, with one sleek bare shoulder pressed against his jacket. The perfume she wore was light and familiar. One of her large jet earrings was tangled in her hair. The stones glistened like black diamonds, reflecting an odd faceted light on her pale skin.

Dan grinned sheepishly when their eyes met. Her smile was stunningly warm. Instinctively he looked away. "Hey, I'm not saying a thing," he kidded her. "I'm not even looking at you."

"Was it that bad?" Her voice sounded exactly as he'd imagined it would—soft, rich, confident. There was just the right apologetic tone to the words, not obsequious, not flippant, a classy little chuckle underneath them.

"Put it this way," he said, "I'm glad I wasn't on the receiving end."

"I hate the way some guys think they have a right to come on like that."

He wanted to agree with her. He felt like a traitor to Jimmy. She was still smiling. He said, "Jimmy's okay. A little insecure . . . like the rest of us—"

There was a pause. She was watching him with evident interest. He didn't move away. She was really sensational looking. She must have been in her thirties, he figured. She dressed younger, stylishly trendy. But she could get away with it. No problem.

"I'm Dan Gallagher," he said, at last.

She held out a well-tended cool hand. "Alex Forrest," she said, shaking firmly. A touch of class.

"Alex." He tested it. Cleared his throat. "What's your connection here?"

"I work for Robbins and Hart. I'm an associate editor. . . ." What a dazzling smile. Clean, rich teeth. "And you?" she asked.

"I'm with Miller, Goodman and Hurst. I do all your legal work. I'm surprised I've never seen you around."

She took a sip of her champagne. "I just joined them a couple of weeks ago," she said leisurely.

Something across the room caught Dan's attention. He looked up. Beth was near the door with Hildy and Jimmy. She signaled to him that they all wanted to leave.

Dan nodded, indicated that he was on his way. Then he turned to Alex and shrugged apologetically. "I've got to go."

"Is that your wife?" she asked. Same fabulous smile, same classy bemused chuckle under the words.

"Yes."

"Well," she teased lightly, "you'd better run along then."

"See you around sometime," he said. "Very nice to meet you." And it was, Dan Gallagher thought as he made his way back to Beth. It felt very nice to be chatted up by a gorgeous, classy blonde who clearly didn't feel that charitable to every man at the party.

Very nice.

—— 2 ——

He saw her again the next day.

It was a warm September Saturday. It began filled with sunlight and ended up steamy, streets slick with rain, smoke rising from sewer grates.

It began early with him piling Beth, Ellen, their bags, and Ellen's bicycle into the station wagon. And hauling Quincy out of the car. Ellen had wanted the big dog to go with them, up to Beth's parents' place. Beth had wanted Ellen to spit out her gum and get into the car. And Dan had wanted Beth not to fall in love with the first house the real estate agent showed her.

"If you like it when you see it, don't say

anything, for God's sake," he cautioned her, "or we can't negotiate."

"Ellen, are you chewing gum again?" she had said.

"You know, we can't afford this house," Dan reminded her.

"No harm in looking, is there? It's just up the road from Mom and Dad—"

"That's another good reason for not buying it," he'd teased her.

The truth was he liked Beth's parents. They were the original "decent, hardworking people." Of course, their hard work had paid off a bit better than most. Beth's dad, Howard, now retired, called himself an old "adman." The truth was he had owned the agency. Her mother had been a model in her time, a cover girl of some renown in the early fifties. There had even been a Penn print of her included in the fashion photographer's one-man show at the Modern.

On the surface, Gallagher's own family looked pretty much like the Rogersons. But there were differences. The Rogersons were suburban, the Gallaghers city folks. Dan had grown up in Manhattan. His father, Frank, was a journalist instead of an adman. He'd traveled a great deal, been away from home a lot. But then so, in his own way, had Howard

Rogerson, who'd put in twelve-hour days and whose social life, Beth said, had consisted of entertaining clients.

Dan's mother, Lilly, was less beautiful than Joan Rogerson and more vulnerable—though through his childhood she had seemed invincibly strong and happy to him. It was the divorce, he thought, that had undone her. She'd been close to fifty then. If it didn't break her heart, it broke her spirit, Dan thought.

She lived in northern California now, near her older sister, Kate, who was also divorced. His father lived in Paris with his Vietnamese mistress.

"I didn't hear that," Beth had said, sliding into the station wagon.

"Hear what?"

"That crack about my parents. Anyway, darling, let's not worry about it now, okay? I haven't even seen the place yet. I may not even like it."

"I love you," he said.

She cocked her head at him. She looked puzzled for a moment, then she beamed one of her terrific smiles at him. "I'm glad," she said. "We're going to miss you. You won't forget to walk Quincy, will you? I'm sorry, Quincy," she said to the dog, who was straining at his leash trying to climb into the backseat.

"He wants to go with us, Mommy."

"Hey, what about me?" Dan demanded. "I want to go with you, too. But you don't see me whimpering and tap dancing all over the upholstery, do you? At least, not yet."

"Oh, you!" Ellen said, eyes twinkling just like Beth's.

He kissed them both.

"Have a good meeting," Beth called, throwing him a final kiss.

Ellen waved at her window. " 'Bye, Daddy."

"Say hello to Grandma and Grandpa!"

And they were off. And he and Quincy lumbered into Central Park for a Saturday-morning jog.

It started clouding up about noon. By the time Dan left the apartment for his afternoon meeting at Robbins and Hart, the sky was striped with scudding clouds. He'd planned to walk through the park to the publishing house, but decided against it. He grabbed one of the half-dozen little black umbrellas stuck in the hall closet. He must have bought three times that number over the years from the Nigerians who appeared all over Manhattan to hawk them at the first drop of rain.

Catching a cab to Fifty-third and Fifth, Dan made it into the Robbins and Hart building while the sun and clouds fought it out overhead.

Bob Drimmer, his assistant Bill, R&H's public relations director, and a couple of guys from the legal department were having coffee and bagels in the conference room. Drimmer's British secretary, Melissa, handed out yellow pads and freshly sharpened pencils.

She greeted Dan in her cheerful, semiformal way. "Mr. Gallagher," she said with a pert nod.

"Miss Simmons," Gallagher teased her.

"Melissa," she corrected him. "Really, I prefer it."

"Dan," he said, knowing she'd call him Mr. Gallagher anyway.

"Hi, Dan," Drimmer said, looking up awkwardly, hindered by the neck brace.

He knew everyone there. They exchanged hellos and is-it-raining-yets.

"Sorry to ruin your weekend," Drimmer said. "Please give my apologies to your lovely wife."

Dan laughed, remembering Drimmer's momentary infatuation with Beth. "No problem, she's used to it. How's your neck? Any better?"

"Please. Don't ask." Drimmer shook his head stiffly. His shoulders shifted with the effort. "Henry Noonan's out of town, so I've asked Alex Forrest to stand in for him at the meeting." Drimmer swiveled, searching the faces at the table. "Has anybody seen Alex?"

It didn't register right away. The name sounded familiar, but Dan didn't even think female until Melissa said, "She's on her way." And even then, he didn't think blonde.

"While we're waiting," Dan said, concentrating on choosing the perfect bagel, "you want to tell us what happened to your neck, Bob?"

There was an outbreak of suppressed laughter, throat clearing, and coughing.

"That's cute, very cute." Drimmer tried to shake his head again. This time he winced in pain. "I was planting geraniums," he began in exasperation.

Dan could hardly contain his laughter. At that moment, however, Alex Forrest came through the door, slightly out of breath. He recognized her at once. Her quick, delighted smile told him she shared his pleasure and surprise.

He was wearing an ancient Izod and weekend cords. She was as slinky as she had been last night, in a two-piece white suit with no blouse to get between the jacket and her skin.

"Sorry," she said, "I was just getting the file."

"Dan, this is Alex Forrest, our new associate editor."

"We've met before," he told Drimmer.

She offered her hand and he rose slightly from his chair to shake it. "Hello, again. Hi, Bill." She nodded, businesslike, to Bob Drimmer's assistant, and the others.

"All right," Drimmer said, starting the meeting. "If we may. Okay, Dan—"

"Okay, here's the deal. . . . You want to publish a novel in which one of the characters is a senator from New Jersey who fools around. A congressman from Ohio claims the character is based on him and has filed an injunction against publication."

"Look," Drimmer interrupted, "the congressman's bald, this guy has hair, he's from another state, for Chrissakes. . . . Look, if we can't sell these books, we're screwed."

Dan shrugged. "Well, that's all fine. But if I'm going to go into court and prove the senator isn't based upon this congressman, I have to know the truth. Now, strictly speaking, between these walls, did the author have an affair with Mr. Ohio or not?"

Drimmer looked nervous. He glanced at Alex, then nodded imperceptibly, giving her permission to speak.

"Yes, she did," Alex said. She was all business. Then a small smile played across her lips. "However . . . she's also had affairs with a lot of other politicians. Any one of them could make this claim. She swears the character's fictitious. I just got off the phone with her."

"And you believe her?" Dan asked.

She weighed it, smiling unflinchingly at him. "Yes," she finally said. "I believe her."

Dan took a big bite of his bagel. He thought for a minute. When he looked up again, she smiled at him and signaled that he had a dab of cream cheese on his nose. He wiped it off with a napkin and smiled back gratefully.

"Good," Drimmer said. "Now that *that*'s on the table, let's see if we can move ahead. How soon can we have this injunction lifted? I've got twenty-five thousand books in a warehouse gathering dust."

The sound of thunder punctuated the strategy session. Then the pebbly noise of rain hit the conference room's tinted windows. Far below, they could hear, faintly, the hissing noise of cars sweeping along the rain-slick streets.

By the time the meeting was over and Dan hit the lobby, it was pouring outside. He pulled the folding umbrella from his briefcase and snapped it open. It lasted about five steps out into the driving rain. A gust caught it as he dashed to the curb.

Abruptly the rods tore through the flimsy material.

"Son-of-a-bitch," he muttered, and simultaneously discovered Alex Forrest laughing at him.

She'd been standing about two feet away, searching the street for a cab. She was dry and calm under her sturdy, dependable umbrella. He'd have been willing to bet it held a pedigree from Abercrombie's or Hunting World.

She approached him, smiling. "Is it made in Taiwan?" she chided.

He played sheepish. "Hey, look, these are tough to find. . . . No kidding. Don't laugh." Then he gave up and tossed the umbrella into the trash bin. "Do you believe this?" he asked, putting his briefcase over his head.

He searched the street for a cab.

"Oh, wait," Alex cried, spotting one caught in traffic halfway down the block. "Here, I've got one."

"Hey, buddy, come on!" Dan waved his arm, flagging the cab. "How about giving us a break!"

They craned their necks hopefully but the driver turned on his OFF DUTY sign and whisked past them.

"Oh, come on!" Alex wailed.

"Is this incredible?" Dan said.

They stood there, getting wetter as the rain intensified. Finally he said, "This is hopeless. Do you want to get a drink someplace until it stops?"

She considered it. Then took his arm. "Yeah. Sure," she said. "Come on."

Dan had wanted a beer, but he'd acquiesced when Alex Forrest suggested sharing a small carafe of wine. The restaurant she'd led them to wasn't a beer kind of joint anyway. It was an intimate and opulent little bistro in the East Sixties.

The place sported wood-paneled walls and etched-glass partitions. There were glowing brass fixtures atop the banquettes, and fresh flower arrangements so lush and large they would dwarf small children. The one at the end of the polished mahogany bar was easily as tall as Ellen, Dan Gallagher mused. Still, the place was inviting, elegant, cool, and dry. Not unlike the woman sitting beside him, he thought.

Just then, a man came in from the street, drenched and cursing.

"Pretty rotten out there," Alex said, finishing her wine.

Dan glanced at the clock behind the bar. Close to six. It would be impossible to find a cab now. Even if it hadn't been pouring out there, it was the witching hour. Everyone was going somewhere in the rain. Matinee matrons and serious shoppers heading home. Moviegoers starting out. Kids returning from their Saturday self-improvement classes at the city's cultural meccas—the music apprecia- tion concerts at Lincoln Center, art tours at the Modern and Met, lecture series at the Museum of Natural History, drawing, danc- ing, singing, and acting classes, football scrimmages, gymnastics practice. The hu- man comedy was out there splashing and hassling for transportation.

Everyone was going somewhere. He'd told Beth he'd try to make it up to Mt. Kisco tonight. He needed to get home, walk the mighty Quince, then get over to Grand Cen- tral Station. The trains ran regularly up until midnight. They ran later than that tonight, he remembered, because it was Saturday. Gallagher was in no particular hurry.

"Want another one?" he asked, offering Alex the last of the wine.

"Sure." She looked at her watch while he emptied the carafe's dregs into her glass. "I'm starving," she said. "Have you got to be anywhere?"

"No . . . you want to eat?"

She gave him a "yes" smile, then hopped off the stool. "I have to make a phone call," she said.

Dan watched her go. He was impressed with her looks, with the lithe body, the soft white summer suit, the cascade of blonde curls. Men at the bar followed her with their eyes and women with their envy. He watched her, intrigued with her moves and the developing situation.

Alex Forrest. She liked him. She was—if not exactly warm—bright and responsive and, face it, sexy as hell.

He had nothing to do, nowhere to go. It was a boring rainy Saturday night.

Beth and Ellen were up at her folks' place. The two of them were probably reading, curled up together in the living-room window seat, facing the lake. Or they might be helping Joan pull together one of her dynamite dinners.

Dan missed them suddenly. He reached automatically into his pocket to look for change. He wanted to phone them.

He didn't, however, want to hear right now that Beth had found the perfect house. He wasn't sure he really wanted to live in Westchester. He wondered what Arthur had been hinting at last night. Anxiety played a familiar palpitating tattoo in his chest. He hated change. He had everything he'd ever wanted now, here, right in New York City, where he'd lived his whole life.

Leave well enough alone.

Alex was coming back from the pay phone. He paid their bar tab and told the headwaiter that they'd like a table.

The restaurant began to get busy. The steady hum of conversation grew louder. They sat opposite each other at a snug table for two near the window. The rain had not let up. Dan watched it for a moment.

"It's a fascinating profession, isn't it?" Alex said.

"The law?"

He turned back to face her. She nodded. She looked relaxed and friendly now. She looked familiar, like someone he'd known for a long time, Dan thought. She was easy to talk to. Not easy to impress, but a good listener. She nodded at all the right places, smiled with recognition at shared ideas and feelings, laughed easily now.

Her warmth and acceptance fueled his good humor. He began performing with zest for her. He pulled out his favorite old stories and freshened them up for her benefit.

"It has its moments," he said.

"What was the strangest case you ever handled?" Alex asked, giving him the perfect segue into one of his best anecdotes.

"Strangest? Well the truth is I never actually handled it, but the strangest one I ever came *near* was when my parents decided to get divorced and my mother asked me to represent her."

"No," Alex said.

He laughed. "Hard to believe."

"You're kidding."

Dan didn't miss a beat. "That's what I said to her. 'What do you mean?' she told me. 'You know what a bum the guy is. . . .' "

"No!"

He nodded. "No kidding. 'You've been an eyewitness to this marriage for twenty-nine years,' she tells me. Can you imagine this—from my own mother?"

"How did you get out of it?" Alex asked. "What did you do?"

Dan stole a glance at the street. The rain was letting up, at last. A thick mist was replacing the downpour. "Well," he said, smiling at Alex Forrest, "you can't just turn down your mother. I escaped on a technicality."

She laughed. It made him feel good. He liked that laugh. He liked women who smiled a lot and could laugh aloud.

A busboy moved in to clear the table. Dan leaned back out of his way.

"What was the technicality?" she pressed him when the boy had gone.

"I told her I didn't practice family law—which was true. She bought it," he said.

"You're making this up."

"I wish I were," he said, shaking his head. "Who could make that up?"

Alex took out a cigarette. He lit it for her, then tried, unsuccessfully, to signal a waiter.

"It takes a special touch," he kidded as one went by, studiously ignoring him. "As you can see, I have a lot of pull here—"

"Clearly," she said.

"Oh, miss."

"You seem to have better luck with women," she said as a waitress responded to his signal.

"You want coffee?" he asked Alex. She nodded. "Can we get two coffees?"

The waitress went off. Alex watched him with a little smile. She offered him a cigarette.

"No, thanks. It's funny," Dan said, "being a lawyer's a lot like being a doctor. People let you in on their innermost secrets."

He thought he'd tell her about one of Jimmy Lawrence's juicy divorce cases. No names, of course. Just the incredible facts and how the wife in the matter had laid them out shamelessly for Jimmy. And how she'd paused in the middle of this practically porn novel she was reciting deadpan to ask Jimmy what was wrong with his ears. What was wrong with his ears, Jimmy had told him, was that they were burning. Literally. They were bright red with embarrassment. His whole face was flushed, but his ears were so hot they stung as if they'd been severely sunburned.

"You must have to be discreet." She caught him off guard. "With secrets," she added.

"That's right."

She smiled. "Are you?"

"Am I what?"

"Discreet."

"Oh," he said ironically, "I'm very discreet."

"Me, too," she said matter-of-factly. But she held his gaze a beat too long.

The waitress returned with their coffee. "Cream?" she offered Alex.

"Black," Alex said coldly, without taking her eyes off Dan.

The waitress turned to him with the cream. He smiled awkwardly, and shook his head. He assured her he was fine, thank you.

Alex seemed relieved when the girl left. Dan offered her sugar. She said, "Not for me," and watched him as he stirred some into his cup.

There was a momentary lull.

It made him uncomfortable. She was just

staring at him. She looked extraordinarily good. Confident and happy. Those pale green eyes just stroked his face. Her smile was enigmatic, peaceful. Satisfied, that was how she looked, as if she had everything she wanted, and he was part of it.

"You know what really surprises me," he said very softly. Then he cleared his throat. "Can I ask you something? I don't understand . . . I mean, you were free. Why don't you have a date . . . Saturday night? Someone as attractive as you—"

"I did have a date," she replied in the rich, throaty voice that suddenly made him think of last night, of her perfume and how her bare shoulder had pressed against him at the bar. "I stood him up. That was the phone call I made."

Dan was flattered, as she'd no doubt intended him to be. He couldn't suppress a triumphant little smile.

She noticed and laughed lightly. "Does that make you feel good?"

He was going to finesse the answer, then he changed his mind and laughed. "It doesn't make me feel bad," he admitted.

"So. Where's your wife?"

It took him by surprise. He fumbled with his words, and almost choked on his coffee.

"My wife? She's . . . in the country. For the weekend . . . visiting her parents."

"And here you are—" she began, coolly.

He held up his hand as if to protest his innocence, but Alex shook her head. "Being a naughty boy," she continued.

"We're having dinner. Is that a crime?"

She smiled. "Not yet."

Jesus, Gallagher thought. He tried to hold her gaze, but lost the battle and found his eyes falling to the smooth skin inside the draped V-shaped lapels of her jacket. The warm rise of her breasts was beginning to get to him. He felt himself stir like a schoolboy. The rest of her looked tanned compared with the velvety pale flesh that now showed above the first button of her white jacket.

"Will it be?" he asked her, trying to keep his tone light. She might be teasing him. Maybe he was reading too much into this.

"I don't know," she said. "What do you think?"

"I think . . ." He smiled and caught her eye again. Then he knew she wasn't kidding. She was considering him. She was serious. She was measuring him against her own desire. His body knew it before his mind did. A surge of blood swept into him. "I think it's going to be up to you," he said.

Alex nodded. "Well . . . I can't say yet. I

haven't made up my mind. I can't decide."
She held his gaze, then smiled.

"At least you're honest."

"We were attracted to each other at the party. That's obvious. You're on your own for the night." She was laying it all out for him. She took a drag on her cigarette and let the smoke out leisurely. Then she melted him with one of her wide open, confident smiles. "We're adults," she said.

Dan nodded. "Let's get the check."

— 3 —

A cab pulled up as they stepped outside the restaurant. Two men and a woman got out. Alex and Dan slid into the backseat. The driver was a heavily unshaven Greek, according to his permit. Alex gave him an address. In a partitioned world of his own, he drove, accompanied by a tinny transistor suspended from his rearview mirror.

The cab careened at top speed along the pothole-studded streets. In the back, Alex and Dan exchanged glances, laughed, and shook their heads at how strange it was, what they were doing.

His jacket lay across his lap. He was very aware of her body. He could feel her heat. Her thigh rested lightly against his. The silky sleeve of her white suit brushed his bare arm.

Alex drew a cigarette from her purse and handed him her lighter.

"Where the hell do you live?" he said. "I never heard of that street."

She steadied his hand as he lit her cigarette. "The meat district," she said, holding his hand a beat too long, smiling into his eyes.

He laughed.

Outside, a fiery glow tinted the heavy air. The twilight streets were slick after the rain. Puddles reflected the garish neon of the city.

Alex threw back her head when she exhaled. The arc of suddenly exposed pale flesh at her throat startled Dan, drove him nuts. He wanted to pounce on it, press his lips against it. He wanted to run his tongue up and down her throat.

With a jolt, he began to harden. He rearranged the jacket on his lap. She caught him and smiled.

"The meat district?" Dan shook his head.

A sudden lurch threw Alex harder against him. Her jacket top bowed. She was not wearing a bra. Her breasts were plump and perfect, milky white. She had a tan.

She touched his arm. A sweet deep pain pulsed in him at the shock of her fingertips on his skin, at the sight of her breasts pushed together as she reached for him.

A trickle of moisture moved slowly down her chest, toward the V of her breasts. Dan watched it. He followed it with his eyes and heightened senses as it slid toward her cleavage. He could feel himself growing under the jacket. He cleared his throat and laughed as he adjusted himself.

Alex Forrest put her hand on top of his as it rested on his crotch. She stroked the back of his hand for a moment. The feeling ran right through Dan, through the back of his hand to his palm, to the thickened organ straining beneath his jacket.

Dan surrendered. He put his head back against the seat and closed his eyes. Whatever she wanted was okay with him. Whatever she wanted to do.

It was as if she had read his mind.

Alex Forrest lifted his hand and placed it on her chest, up near her throat, where the trickle of moisture had begun its descent. She guided his hand slowly down along her amazing moist skin, down to the plump rise of her breasts. She dug his fingers into her cleavage. She ran his hand up and down the perspiration-wet cleft.

Dan moaned. He turned his head and fell onto her, pressing his face between her breasts.

He seized her slender waist and buried his face against her and licked the salty wetness. She was breathing hard. Her chest was heaving. He sucked and bit her breasts.

The cab's reckless speed and wild lurching became an extension of his will. Alex pulled his hair. She ran her fingers through his thick hair and scratched his head with her long nails. She tugged at his hair.

"Dan . . ." He heard the laughter in her husky voice. "We're here. Stop. Wait. Dan."

"Jesus Christ," he said.

"We're here. Stop here."

He sat back. Alex leaned forward. "It's up here on the left," she told the driver.

"Jesus Christ," Dan said. "Where are we?"

He followed her inside a dilapidated-looking loft building. The elevator was ancient, a huge metal cage. Dan leaned back against its iron gates as it made its creaky ascent. Alex stepped between his splayed legs. She wrapped her arms around his neck and pressed her body into his. He began hardening again, immediately.

He followed her like a dog, off the elevator, down a narrow dark corridor, and into her loft. She had a key hidden on top of a gas meter just outside her door. The spacious apartment was more like what he'd expected of her. It was sparsely but tastefully furnished, partitioned with walls of books and records. She took his hand and led him into the kitchen, which was literally a step up from the rest of the place. "I'll fix us some coffee," she said. "Go on, look around."

He wandered through the place. He saw where her bed was located. It was up against a brick wall. Nice lamp. Piles of books on the bedside table. Telephone on the floor. He followed the phone cord to the living-room area and examined her records and tapes. Good collection. Eclectic. Lots of opera. His father would have liked her.

He turned back toward the kitchen. She was rinsing something at the sink. She turned as if she had felt his eyes on her back. She looked over her shoulder at him. Her long, blond hair was wild and full. Her face was damp and flushed. She smiled at him. Her green eyes fastened on him like hands. They caressed his face and then his body. They drew him toward her.

There was a pot of coffee beginning to boil on the stove. He lowered the light under it as he moved past.

Alex smiled approvingly. "Thank you," she said.

He stepped in front of her. She put her arms around his neck again and, again, she moved toward him, rubbing her full body against his, clinging to him.

The tap water was still running in the sink. Dan leaned forward to shut it. Alex Forrest was wedged between him and the kitchen counter. Her thighs were strong against him. Her belly was firm and round. She pressed into him, smiling. Her nostrils widened, her eyes closed. Her wild blond hair framed a face tilted to his in perfect pleasure.

She rubbed herself from side to side against his growing hardness. He forgot about the water and grabbed a handful of her hair, instead. He pulled on her hair until she arched her back so that her long pale neck was exposed to him as it had been in the taxi cab. Dan bit her throat lightly. He ran his tongue along it, from her clavicle to her chin. Her skin was salty. He sucked her neck. She shuddered and clung more tightly to him. He ran his tongue up over her chin, then touched her lips with his tongue. He kissed her. It began gently, but as his tongue prodded her mouth, she closed her lips around it and began to suck on it. He kissed her savagely then, biting her lips and tongue.

Alex panted and shuddered. When he lifted her up roughly and sat her on the lip of the sink, she gasped. Her straight skirt bound her thighs. She tore at it, trying to free her legs. Gallagher shoved back the fabric and struggled with her panties until her bare ass rested on the counter.

She unbuttoned her jacket. He pulled it back off her shoulders and she pushed his head down onto one of her breasts. While she struggled free of the clothing, he sucked on her nipple, feeling it grow and harden in his mouth. He bit it gently. Alex thrust her breast harder at him. And harder again, until he took the nipple between his teeth and sucked on it ravenously. She leaned back. Her hands bracing herself in the sink accidentally turned the faucet up full force. Alex caught the water in her hand and splashed his face with it. Her breast was in his mouth and she fed him water with her wet hands.

She wrapped her legs around him while he was trying to undo his pants. He had to reach between her thighs to unfasten his zipper. She rubbed herself against his wrist and his hands as he tried to pull his pants down. She was very wet. She rubbed against him rhythmically. He was losing control.

He scooped her up off the rim of the sink, and wrapped her legs around his hips as his pants fell to his ankles. He struggled clumsily with her, stumbling from the kitchen to the bedroom.

His pants, which were still gathered around

his ankles, threatened to trip him up, but he managed to make it to the bed. They fell on it together. Dan kicked his pants off, at last. He rolled her over, lifted her onto him, and—on his knees—rammed into her. During the wild rolling and pushing that followed, they got closer and closer to the edge of the bed. With the final thrust, they fell on the floor, groaning, laughing, exhausted.

Eventually they dragged themselves back onto the bed. He was still breathing hard. She was gasping for breath, but smiling. "That was great . . ." she managed to say.

He was wiped out. He didn't look at her. He didn't even bother to open his eyes. "Thank God," he said.

They lay side by side, slowing down, beginning to breathe easily again. After a while, Alex nuzzled his arm. "Are you feeling energetic?" she asked.

Dan laughed. "What did you have in mind?"

"Want to go dancing?"

He turned his head toward her, squinting incredulously. She shrugged, smiled, sat up. She was serious.

Forty-five minutes later they were bumping and pumping to a throbbing Afro-Latin beat at a downtown club packed with serious dancers. The air was thick with noise and sweat. Alex's face was damp with perspiration. The blouse she'd changed into was soaked, nearly transparent in places.

"You're a great dancer," she shouted above the din.

Her blouse stuck to her. Her breasts showed through in wet, pink patches. Dan could see the rubbery darkness of her nipples bouncing against the wet fabric. "What?" he called.

Alex caught him staring. "I said," she shouted hoarsely. "Forget it." She shrugged with a big, laughing smile and exposed a breast.

Dan looked quickly around. No one had even noticed. Serious dancers. She'd done it for him. Just for him.

There was a distant blush of dawn on the horizon when they left the club. The night air was wonderful. The streets were deserted, cool, and shining after the rain.

They walked for a while, then hailed a cab uptown. Dan fell asleep in the backseat. Alex woke him and he dug, automatically, into his pocket to pay the driver. "It's okay. It's done," Alex said.

She took his hand and dragged him out of the cab and up the steps into the loft building. While they waited for the elevator, she kissed him. It was a lazy, sleepy kiss. Her lips tasted like rain. Like ocean spray. Salty, cool, and wet.

Dan's shirt was wet. Her blouse was wet. Her breasts pressed into him better than bare breasts, alive and straining suddenly, through tired silk and cotton. He put his arms around her and they rolled tiredly into the huge elevator cage. Dan fell back against the wall. The metal cables creaked and droned. The elevator rose slowly. The floors moved past in slow motion, one after the other, horizon after horizon, like the slow-motion roll of a giant television screen.

Alex slumped up against him, holding his hand. Absently she stroked his hand and arm. He closed his eyes. She kissed them, then kissed his neck, gently licking the hollow where his neck and chest intersected. Slowly her hands began to move over him, from his chest, his nipples, to his abdomen, down over the taut muscles of his groin. Slowly she began to stroke him. She pulled open his shirt and licked his nipple. She pushed her hand into his pants and teased him with her fingers.

Dan groaned as Alex Forrest undid his belt and rubbed him gently with her palm. As he hardened, she increased her touch, curled him into her palm, turned her palm into a fist. He was breathing hard. "Jesus, holy shit," he gasped, rocking in her hand. Suddenly she groped for the button to stop the elevator. She slammed it with her free hand. The car jolted to a halt.

Dan heard a door slam somewhere in the building. He heard footsteps approaching the elevator. Alex was sinking to her knees in front of him, pulling down his trousers.

He saw a man approaching the elevator. The loft hallways were dark. The elevator was comparatively well lit. They were inside the metal cage. Alex was on her knees in front of him. Dan was standing there, with his trousers down around his thighs. She must have heard the guy, too. She had to have sensed him staring at them. But it didn't stop her. She took him into her mouth and he bucked hard against her lips, right there under the glaring bare light.

Dan reached blindly, frantically, searching for the button to start the elevator. He found it, hit it. The car started up. He grabbed Alex's arms and hurled her to her feet suddenly. He turned her around, slammed her against the wall of the elevator. She held on to the bars while he tore open her blouse and fumbled with her zipper. She gasped when he entered her, when he wrapped her thighs around his hips. The elevator clanged metallically as her buttocks beat against the side wall. The cables whined, the shaft reverberated with their frantic movements, their gasps and cries.

Outside her door, Alex fumbled for the hidden key on top of the gas meter. Her arm shook as she reached for it. She handed the key to Dan. He propped himself up with one hand against the doorjamb and unlocked her apartment.

She was asleep when he left. Daylight had awakened him in her bed. He left a note for her on the end table next to the bed and quietly let himself out of her apartment.

When he got uptown, Quincy was asleep against the front door. The big dog stirred at the sound of the key in the lock. Dan could hear the dull thud of Quincy's tail beating the floor expectantly, and then the clicking of his heavy nails against the parquet.

"Good boy, Quincy," he said, scratching the dog's head affectionately. "Yeah, I'm going to take you out in a minute." He looked over at the answering machine. The message indicator was blinking. "We'll go in a minute, boy. Yes, we will," he promised.

He rewound the messages. There were a couple of clicks before Beth's voice came on: *Hi. What happened to you? . . . I tried you earlier. I guess you're not back . . . I'm going to bed now, so call me in the morning.*

The sound of her voice, the easy intimacy, the familiarity, brought him home again. He'd been disoriented in the cab coming uptown. Anxious and uneasy. As if he didn't quite know where he was going or why. He thought maybe it was the strange quiet of the city early Sunday morning. Or the lack of sleep. The booze maybe. He hadn't had that much to drink, but still he felt hung over.

The machine beeped and rewound. Gallagher erased the message. Then he went into the bedroom and undressed.

On his way to the shower, he stopped in front of the framed photograph of Beth and Ellen that sat on top of his dresser. He loved Beth's face. He missed her, he realized. He was sorry that he'd erased the answering machine message now. He felt like listening to her voice again. Soon, he promised himself, he'd call her. He'd hear her voice again. but first, he needed a long, hot shower.

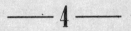

4

"**H**ello? Oh, hello, Dan darling," Beth's mother answered the phone with lively warmth. "We were expecting you." There was a distinctive echo on the line that told Gallagher she was using the cordless phone.

"Yes, I know. I'm sorry I couldn't make it. Where are you," he asked, "out in the garden?"

"No, dear," Joan Rogerson said, "I'm in the greenhouse. Is the phone awful?"

He could picture her with her gardening gloves and sunglasses on; cordless phone in one hand, muddy trowel in the other. "No, it's fine," Dan assured her, smiling.

"Beth and Ellen are outside with Howard. Playing football, I think," Joan said.

"Well, anyway, they've got a football out there. Ellen's on Howard's shoulders. . . . They look happy enough, whatever they're up to. It's a pity you can't make it, dear. We really wanted you to see this house. It's not far. And I know how much you've always liked the area—"

"Well, I'll see it next time."

The area was fine. Terrific, really. Westchester. Mt. Kisco. But it was the Rogersons' home Gallagher had always admired. The house in which Beth had grown up. He remembered how impressed he'd been the first time he saw it—Christ, that had been a dozen years ago—when Beth first brought him home to meet her parents.

"Of course," Joan Rogerson said now. "Hold on, dear. I'll get Beth for you. . . ."

It wasn't just that the house she'd grown up in was this big, rambling *Father Knows Best* kind of place, with bay windows and a couple of working fireplaces and a breakfast nook; or that it was on a lake, though that *had* impressed him, Dan remembered. It was what that home had told him about the Sarah Lawrence girl he'd fallen in love with, the way it reflected and confirmed what he'd thought about Beth Anne Rogerson from the start—that she was the real thing. Warm, loving, and solid.

"Well, hello," Beth said. She sounded breathless, and happy. He could picture her running in from the lawn that sloped down to the lake. "What happened to you?"

"Oh, I ended up having dinner with Bill," he said vaguely.

"You sound like you've got a hangover."

"No," he said, a bit too quickly, too defensively. "I feel fine."

He heard his mother-in-law's voice in the background. "Ellen, be careful!" she was shouting. What happened to Ellen? Is she okay, he wanted to ask.

"How is he?" Beth said, oblivious to whatever it was her mother was cautioning Ellen about.

"He's . . . same as ever," Dan said easily. "You know Bill. Just Bill."

"Is he still with that girl?"

"Well," he wasn't last night." Jesus, what had he gotten himself into? "I think it's over," he said. "He didn't seem to want to talk about it."

"So, are you getting any work done?"

"Yes. I'm working. I'm working very hard."

Beth laughed. "Sounds like it. Listen, there's some of the spaghetti sauce in the fridge if you get hungry."

"Right," Dan said. "How's Ellen doing?"

"She's having the best time. I just hope

Dad survives it. I don't know how to tell you this, honey. . . ." Her tone turned confidential. He braced himself. "She wants a rabbit," Beth whispered.

Dan laughed with relief. "No rabbit!" he fairly shouted. "Honey, this family's going to turn into Noah's goddamn ark. Give her a kiss and no promises, okay?" He missed her suddenly. He missed them both. "When are you coming home?"

"Well," Beth said, "it's getting complicated—"

"How come? What do you mean?"

"There's a problem with the house."

"They sold it?" he asked hopefully.

"Very funny. No. It turns out that we can't see it until late this afternoon. Darling, I'm not up to fighting all that traffic. I thought I'd drive in first thing tomorrow morning."

He was disappointed. "What about Ellen? Doesn't she have school?"

"She's five years old. What's she going to miss, trigonometry?"

"Well. Okay," he capitulated reluctantly. "I'll see you when I get home from work."

"Okay," Beth said. " 'Bye, sweetie."

"Take care, okay?" He didn't want to hang up, but he couldn't think of anything else to say. "Have a good time. Love you a lot," he added, then hung up.

Dan stood there for a moment, staring at

the phone. Almost immediately, it rang again. He picked it up, certain it was Beth calling back.

"What happened?" Alex Forrest said. "I woke up and you weren't there? I hate that."

Dan responded to her cautiously. He spoke with the rote calm that came over him when he was truly rankled. "Didn't you see my note?" Dan asked.

"What note?" Alex lit a cigarette. He heard her inhale. At first he thought she was sighing. Then she blew out the smoke and he recognized the sound. He knew it wasn't despair that he'd heard. She was only smoking. He was relieved, almost grateful.

"I left you a note, by the bed."

After a moment, she said, "Oh . . . that's nice. But I thought we were going to spend today together."

Had he promised her that? Dan searched his memory. Maybe he'd had too much to drink. "I've got so much work," he said.

"Why don't you just come over. I'll cook us lunch."

His eyes lit on Quincy. "I've got this dog to look after," he said. "This dog hasn't been out of the house all day. I can't leave him alone all day."

Alex's petulant tone lifted. "Great." She

laughed. "Bring the dog. I love animals. Come on . . . I'm a terrific cook."

Her laughter was persuasive. "Listen," he said, running out of excuses. "I'd love to, Alex, really, but—"

"Look, do what you have to do and then come over. We can always eat late, if you want." She sounded happy again, reasonable, confident.

"Okay . . . maybe later on," he stalled.

She would not be put off. "Or," she continued brightly, as if she'd just solved all their problems, "you can work here. I won't disturb you." She'd begun to purr again. There it was, that deep, sexy voice. The self-assured little chuckle. "I'll be a good girl, Dan. You'll see."

He flashed on her in the elevator, saw her kneeling in front of him. He laughed. "You don't give up, do you?"

Alex laughed with him. "You should be flattered."

He was. He told her so. "I am flattered," he said. "I really am."

"So . . . ?"

"So . . . Okay. But I'm going to do some work here first. Then I've got to take the dog to the park for a walk—"

"All right," Alex said happily. "I'll meet you at the Eighty-first Street entrance at one o'clock!"

*   *   *

Dan didn't get a whole lot done. The house was too quiet, too empty. He couldn't concentrate. At noon, he'd begun to get restless. He was glad he had somewhere to go.

Alex was sitting on a park bench, feeding peanuts to a couple of panhandling squirrels. He'd never seen her in casual clothes before. She wore them well. Her taste was very similar to Beth's, he noticed. The light corduroy jacket over the dark turtleneck, the faded well-cut jeans with their cuffs rolled at the ankles, the stylish but sensible shoes. She looked younger. She was wearing less makeup. Her wild hair was pinned back.

Her face looked softer and more vulnerable. It lit up when she saw him. She threw the rest of the peanuts onto the ground. The squirrels scattered, then retrenched, more startled than grateful, when she jumped up and took his arm.

"And who's this?" Alex asked, bending to scratch Quincy's head.

They walked briskly, pulled by the big dog toward the meadow where he knew he'd be set free to run.

Alex patted the pocket of the baseball jacket where Dan had stashed Quincy's ball. "Better have that looked at," she said, smiling up at him.

Dan unhooked the dog's leash. "It's nothing fatal," he assured her.

Her pale green eyes sparkled with excitement. Her smile was full and bright. She squeezed his arm. Her happiness was visible, almost feverish. He knew it was because she was with him. He didn't understand it, and decided not to try. It felt good. It excited him.

"Ah, but one never knows with these things," she teased. "One moment, you're feeling fine. Top of the world. You've got everything you've ever wanted—"

Dan laughed and pulled the ball out of his pocket. "Cured," he said, showing it to her.

Alex snatched it from his palm. She tossed it lightly in the air, then snatched it back quickly. She laughed, then threw the ball again.

She had a great arm. The ball arched high above them. Quincy went nuts, racing back and forth under it. He caught it on the second bounce, then grandstanded for a couple of minutes, racing around with it in his mouth. Finally he trotted back to them. Whining with pleasure, he dropped the rubber ball at Dan's feet.

Alex ran backward a couple of yards. "Here," she called. Dan threw the drooly ball to her and Quincy took off with a skid.

They ran through the park, the three of them, playing catch, tossing the ball wildly, randomly, jumping for it, fading back, bumping into one another. Quincy barked and jumped and twice ran off with the ball, stopping only so that they could catch up to chase him again.

"Throw it here," Dan called to Alex.

"No way," she shouted, tucking the ball into the crook of her arm as if it were a football. Head down, she sprinted away.

Quincy caught up with her before Dan did. "Go on! Quincy, cover your man!" Dan shouted. The big dog jumped up and knocked Alex down. The ball flew from her arm. Dan grabbed it a second before Quincy did, and took off with it, running in circles while Quincy jumped and yelped ecstatically at his heels.

Dan passed the ball to Alex, faking out the dog, who continued loping after him.

"Here, Quincy! Hey, I've got it. Over here, Quincy!" Alex hollered. Finally the dog turned and headed for her.

"Oh . . . oh, God," she yelled, exhausted. She gave it her best shot. She threw the ball. It was a puny toss. It lacked distance. Dan sprinted forward to intercept. He and Quincy were on a collision course. The ball bounced toward Dan, who lunged for it, and caught it.

He ran on for a few paces, carried forward by his own momentum. Suddenly he stopped.

His knees buckled under him. He sank slowly to the ground, clutching his chest.

The laughter died in Alex's throat. She started toward him in horror. "Dan . . . ?"

He did not move. Panicked, Alex broke into a run. "Dan!" she shouted. She reached the spot where he lay unconscious. She fell to her knees beside him and shook him gently. He didn't move. "Dan . . . ?" she whispered. "Dan, can you hear me . . . ? Oh, God," she cried. "Oh, shit . . ."

Alex put her head to 'his chest to listen for his heartbeat. "Oh, God . . ." She was terrified. She straightened up.

His eyes fluttered open.

"Dan . . . ?" she whispered.

He winked at her. "Gotcha!" he said.

Alex nearly jumped out of her skin. "You bastard!"

He cracked up. "Your face! You should have seen yourself!"

She was furious. Her face was white with fear and rage. She sat back. Tears sprang to her eyes. "That was a shitty thing to do," she said quietly.

Dan sat up. "Hey, I'm sorry. I was just fooling around."

Alex stared into the distance. Her voice was stony. "My father died of a heart attack. I was seven years old," she said. "It happened right in front of me."

He shook his head numbly. He felt terrible. "Alex. I'm sorry. Really I am . . . That's awful." He didn't know what to say, what to do. "I apologize. If I'd known, I never would have—"

She stared icily at him, watching him squirm. Suddenly she burst out laughing.

He was taken aback. It took him a second or two to catch on. "What?" he mumbled like an idiot. "Your dad's okay? Your father . . . he didn't die? He's alive?"

"Alive and well and living in Phoenix," she said triumphantly.

"Jesus Christ." Dan shook his head ruefully. "Well, you got me, kiddo. Whew!" He was all turned around. He didn't know if he was angry or embarrassed or relieved. "I certainly deserved that one."

He studied her for a moment, trying to decide what it was he felt—as if what she did or felt would tell him. She saw him watching her. She lowered her head for just a moment as if she were uncomfortable. But when she looked up again, she was smiling. We're even, he thought her smile said. Or maybe it was, Don't fuck with me.

By three o'clock, the park was filling with long shadows. There was a chill in the air. Alex and Dan bundled into a cab with the dog and drove downtown. Quincy was excited. He sat between them in the back of the taxi, his tail flicking like a metronome.

At Gansevoort Street, Alex got out of the cab. Quincy followed at her heels, mindlessly, trustingly, without a backward glance. Dan shook his head. Like father, like son, he thought. But once inside the loft, the big dog grew cautious. He padded around nervously, sniffing, poking into corners, burrowing under furniture.

Alex threw off her jacket and riffled through her music collection. She selected a tape, tossed the plastic case down, and put the cassette into the tape deck. Then she hurried to the kitchen.

She'd chosen an opera, Dan realized with pleasure. Perfect. He was in the mood for something sweeping and grand.

Madame Butterfly.

The opening strains triggered an unexpected melancholy in him. One moment he felt warm and safe, the next a quiet loneliness had seized him. He looked out a window of the loft, half expecting to find that the day had turned stormy and grim. It hadn't. The darkness was inside him.

That was when he noticed how restless Quincy had become. Dan called the dog to him and scratched his neck and head. "We're not in Kansas, anymore, kiddo," he said, patting Quincy's leaf-matted belly.

Alex came into the room, wearing an apron, looking efficient and happy. She smiled brightly at him and went directly to the tape deck and turned up the volume of *Butterfly*.

"Let's *hear* it!" she shouted.

The moment of melancholy passed, blown away by the explosion of sound. How nice to be with someone who liked to listen to music loud, Dan thought.

"I hope you like spaghetti," Alex called as she hurried back to the kitchen. "Specialty of the house!"

"Goes with the opera," he said.

Quincy yawned and began following his tail. After a few seconds of circling and sniffing, he finally settled down. "Good boy," Dan said softly, patting the dog's back. Then he walked to the window and looked out across the low rooftops to the river.

Alex returned a little while later carrying plates and silverware and cloth napkins. She set them down on the dining table near the window and went back to the kitchen. Dan began to set the table, but Alex called to him to leave everything alone and just relax. She had everything under control, she said. If she needed help, she'd let him know.

He sat down and tugged free the *New York*

Times, which was half under the coffee table and half under Quincy. It was dated from the day before. He put his feet up and browsed through the paper, listening to the music in lazy contentment.

Alex brought him a bottle of wine and a corkscrew and went back to the kitchen. He uncorked the bottle, took it to the table, and poured two glasses. Then he wandered over to the kitchen area where she was cooking up a storm. He watched her quietly for a minute. "That smells so good," he said.

She turned and saw him standing there. She was practically shrouded in steam from the boiling spaghetti water. She brushed a stray strand of hair from her forehead with the back of her hand. And she smiled at him again, that same big dazzling smile that said, *You do this to me.* And for a second, he saw how his being there changed everything for her, completed a picture. Without him, the music, the steamy kitchen, even the table set with linen napkins, a silver candlestick, and a pot of flowers, were props.

Dan supposed he should be flattered. But it made him feel uncomfortable. He smiled back at her. "Anything else I can do to help?"

"No," Alex said, "no, just make yourself at home. You could put on another tape if you want."

"No, this is great. I love *Madame Butterfly.*"

She was pleased. "Really? It's my favorite opera."

He brought her a glass of wine. "Mine, too," he said, twirling his glass, remembering.

How old had he been when his father had taken him to *Butterfly*? Five or six? Very young. About Ellen's age, he guessed. "It's the first opera I ever heard . . . saw," he corrected himself. "My dad took me to see it . . . at the old Met when I was about five years old."

Alex was intrigued. "Did it make sense at all?"

"Oh, yeah, I got the gist of it." The melancholy returned briefly, like a cloud across the sun.

Alex was watching him. He smiled at her. "I understood about this U.S. sailor setting up house with this Japanese girl—I got all that. . . . But in the last act, after he left her and my father told me that she was going to kill herself, I was terrified. I freaked out. And climbed right under the seat." Dan stopped and listened to the record. "Here," he said, suddenly. "Listen. Right here, isn't it?"

He looked at Alex. She nodded. They listened for moment.

"Funny," he continued.

"What?"

"I remember it as being one . . . well, it had to be one of the few times my dad was really nice to me . . . comforting me at *Madame Butterfly*."

He shook his head and smiled at her again. Jesus, he thought, she looks like she's going to cry. Dan took a drink and turned away. He felt like a jerk. What had made him think about all that? Well, the music, obviously. But why had he talked about it?

He saw the concern on Alex's face.

"I'm sorry," he said.

Maybe they'd had too much to drink. Dan remembered pouring the last of the wine into Alex's glass.

The sun had almost set. The window near the dining table was lit with the day's final brilliance. In the fiery twilight, they finished their dinner. Alex's hair was wildly silhouetted against the light. Her face was pensive, almost sad.

She hadn't noticed that he'd refilled her glass. She wasn't aware that he was staring at her until he said, "What? . . . What are you thinking about?"

Then she blinked, and smiled, and shook her head. "I'm wondering . . . why are all the interesting guys always married?"

He cataloged the "all." Should he have been stung by it? Had he imagined he was special?

"Maybe that's what makes them interesting?" he suggested. "Why they're interesting to you—the fact that you can't have them."

"How long have you been married?"

"Nine years," he answered.

"Have you got kids?" She'd leaned forward and put her elbows on the table. She rested her chin in her palms.

"Yes," Dan said. "A five-year-old girl."

She smiled wistfully. "Sounds pretty good."

"Yes. Well, I'm a lucky guy."

"So what are you doing here?" she asked.

He felt himself flush. Instinctively he tugged at his collar, and he laughed uncomfortably. "Boy," he said, shaking his head. "You sure know how to ask them."

"No," she said. "I really want to know." She sat up and ran her finger around the rim of her wineglass. "Look, I had a wonderful time last night. I'd like to see you again. Is that so terrible? So awful?"

"No," Dan said gently. "I just don't think it's possible, Alex. Really. This is very unusual for me. I don't do this."

"It's strange. I feel like I already know you." She sighed. "I guess I just want to know where I stand."

Dan placed his napkin on the table and cleared his throat. He looked her squarely in the eye. His heart had begun to pound. "I think you're terrific," he began. She was watching him with dull eyes. She knew what was coming. She had heard it before. She had heard it all before. He pressed on. "But I'm married. What can I say? I don't know what else to say."

"Just my luck, I guess," she said after a moment. Then she raised her glass ironically and drank, not quite covering her disappointment.

It was time for him to leave. And he wanted to. But he hadn't the heart, or maybe it was the guts, to push away from the table just then and excuse himself. What was he supposed to do, to say? *It's been fun. Thank you.*

Alex Forrest looked crestfallen suddenly. The spirited strength and confidence he'd admired, had even depended on, seemed to be draining from her before his eyes. He pushed back his chair and she flinched as though he'd hit her. "You're not going, are you? Not yet?" she said.

He walked over to her and stroked her hair. "Alex . . ." he began.

She grabbed his hand and kissed it. She got to her feet and put her arms around his neck and pressed her body into his. "I hate good-byes," she said, nuzzling his neck. "I'm no damn good at them. It's so unfair, Dan. I mean, I know you. I feel as though I really know you. I do, don't I? I know this," she said, running her hand over his body.

"Yeah, you do," he said, trying to lighten things up.

"Yeah, I do," she whispered. Her hands moved over him. "I'm going to miss this, and this. . . . I'm going to miss you so. So much," she said, stroking him.

He took her shoulders and held her at arm's length. And laughed. "Jesus," he said.

She looked at him mischievously. "What's up?" she asked with mock innocence.

What was up, of course, was him. Once again his body had responded to her touch. She raised her shoulders, resisting his grip. "You're hurting me," she said softly.

Dan hesitated, reluctant to release her.

"You can if you want to," Alex said. "I just want to make love again. Any way you want. Whatever you want. You can hurt me if you want to, Dan, but you don't have to."

He let go of her.

She led him into her bedroom.

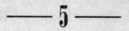

5

Dan woke up naked, under the sheets. Alex was propped up on one elbow, watching him, staring down at him tenderly.

The fading evening light cast voluptuous shadows through the window. For a moment he didn't know where he was. He looked at his watch.

"Shit!" he said, and swung his legs out of the bed.

"What are you doing?" Alex gasped.

He pulled on his shirt. "I have to go."

"What for? I thought you said she didn't get back till tomorrow—"

"Look," he said patiently, "there are things I have to do. I've got to go home."

"You know . . . I don't think I like this," she said angrily.

"Like what?"

She sat up and pulled the sheet around herself. "The way you keep running off every time we make love."

He looked at her. She was serious. Indeed, there was an edge of almost manic desperation to her voice. Dan sighed. "Alex . . ." he began gently, trying to find a way to take the heat out of the situation. "Whether I leave now or in the morning, the fact is, I've got to go."

He turned to walk toward the bathroom. He was buttoning his shirt.

"Well, you're not going to go now!" she shouted like a petulant child. Suddenly she grabbed his shirt.

It startled him. It drew him up short. "This is . . ." What was he going to say— ridiculous, childish, embarrassing? But she wasn't kidding, and she was very strong. "Stop it," he said, still trying to control his temper. "For Chrissake, Alex. Stop it!"

There was a loud rip as his shirt tore. He couldn't believe it. What the hell was going on here? He whirled to face her. "What's the problem?" he asked angrily. "What are you doing?"

She seemed as startled as he, and as angry. "I'm sorry," she said sarcastically.

"What's the matter with you? Be reasonable, okay?"

"Me be reasonable? What . . . Thank you, good-bye, don't call me, I'll call you."

His face was burning. He ignored the rip and started to button up his shirt again. "You knew all about me," he said with controlled anger. "I didn't hide anything. I thought it·was all understood."

She looked ragged. Her eyes were blazing with anger. "*What* was understood?" she challenged.

He put on his pants. "The opportunity was there and we took it. We're both adults, aren't we?" he said, fastening his belt.

"What is that supposed to mean?" Alex demanded.

"I thought we could have a good time." It sounded lame, even to him.

"No," she responded with quiet fury. "You thought *you'd* have a good time. You didn't stop for a second to think about me."

"This is crazy!" he protested. "You knew the rules—"

She glared at him. "What rules?" she asked contemptuously.

Dan sat down at the edge of the bed. And began to put on his shoes. "Look, Alex." He tried to reason with her. "I like you. I do. I'm not saying if I wasn't with someone else . . . in another time and place . . . that we couldn't have had . . ." What the hell was he trying to say? He was tired, exhausted. "I'm *not free*," he said, finally.

She groaned. "Please! Don't justify yourself. It's pathetic. If you just told me to fuck off, I'd have more respect for you."

Dan looked at her with calm deliberation. "All right. Fuck off," he said.

"Okay . . . And you—" She lashed out with her foot, kicking him off the edge of the bed. "Get out!" Then she scrambled off the bed and ran out of the room.

Dan sat there, on the floor for a minute, staring at the empty doorway. Then he shook his head. He felt like a jerk. And he was still angry. His heart was pumping like mad.

He heard Alex clattering around the kitchen. She was sobbing. He sat there thinking that he should go to her, that he ought to try to calm her down some way. She was sobbing in great, loud gulps.

Adrenaline was still surging through him. He was too wired to help her now. He was too confused. What the hell had happened? How had it gone from fun to fighting so fast? Maybe she was right. Maybe only he had thought it was fun. . . . Was that it? Was that what he'd thought? Fun? No. Not exactly. Excitement? Adventure? Oh, Jesus.

Dan got to his feet. He brushed off his shirt and pants. Maybe it was better this way, he tried to tell himself as he went into the bathroom to wash up. Retribution, quick and clean. You sin. You pay. You get kicked in the ass. It's over.

Alex was hunched over the kitchen sink when Gallagher came in. She was wearing only a T-shirt. He cleared his throat so that he wouldn't startle her. She heard him and dropped something onto the kitchen counter with a metallic clatter.

"Okay, I'm leaving," he said quietly.

Alex turned around. She was smiling, but she looked like hell. Her eyes were red from crying. Her hands were behind her back, as though she needed them to prop her up against the counter.

"Why don't you come here and say good-bye nicely . . ." she said. Her voice broke. It was shot, rough-edged and ragged. She had cried herself raw. "Okay?" she said. "Let's be friends."

Dan found himself moving warily toward her. He didn't want to. He wanted to run. He didn't like the way she looked. Her smile was all wrong. It was more an act of will than a smile. Her lips were quivering. Her pale green eyes darted nervously.

When he was about a foot away, she swooped forward and put her arms around his neck. Instinctively he pulled back, but she held him and kissed him. "I'm sorry if I upset you," she said breathlessly.

"It's okay," Dan said.

Alex kissed him again, more fiercely this time. She held his face in both her hands and kissed him hard on the lips. Then she released him and took a step back. She smiled again, as if having kissed him had been an achievement. There was a triumphant gleam in her eyes as Dan raised a hand to his cheek.

"Your hands are all wet," he said, wiping the side of his face.

He glanced down at his own hand. It was smeared with blood. He didn't understand. He looked to Alex for an explanation. Her smiled disappeared behind a wall of bloodied flesh. She put her hands in front of her face, brandishing her wrists at him. She was laughing uncontrollably, as bright red blood poured from the deep, ugly gashes on her wrists.

"Oh, Jesus Christ!" Dan gasped. "Jesus!" He caught her wrists tightly and dragged her to the sink. He ran cold water over the cuts. Alex winced with pain. Her crazy laughter turned to tears. "Hold on," he urged her. "Keep it under the water. Jesus Christ!"

"I'm sorry . . . I'm sorry!" Alex cried.

"Do you have a first-aid kit?"

She shook her head. Her body was convulsed with sobs. "No," she rasped.

He was beginning to shake. He could feel himself losing it. He kept one arm tight around Alex's heaving body. With his other hand, he held her wrists under the water. "Alex, Alex, listen to me. Have you got a bandage? Have you got anything I can use as a bandage?" He propped her against the sink. "Here. Hold on . . . Hold tight," he instructed. He dashed into her bedroom, flinging open doors and searching frantically through her dresser looking for something to use as a bandage. Finally he found a white shirt and began to tear it into strips.

He bound her wrists and led her into the bathroom. She sat at the side of the tub, her bandaged wrists in her lap, her head bowed, submitting passively to his ministrations. There was blood all over her. Even her pretty blond hair was matted with it.

Dan crouched in front of her adjusting the bandages. "Is that too tight?" he asked gently.

Alex shook her head.

"We've got to go to the hospital, Alex. You may need stitches."

"No," she whispered. "I'm okay. I'm all right, really. I'm fine."

He put a finger under her chin and lifted her head so that he could see her face. He looked into her eyes, as if searching for an explanation. Alex turned her head away.

"Don't look at me like that," she begged. "Why are you looking at me like that?"

He saw her tears begin to brim again. He saw her fight them back.

"Why, Alex? Can you tell me why? Why are you so unhappy?"

She looked at him. She started to speak but couldn't get the words out before she burst into tears. Finally, through her strangled sobs, he heard: "I'm so *alone.*"

The words came out in a protracted, primal wail, a terrible cry of pain. Burying her face in her bandaged hands, Alex began to weep uncontrollably.

Dan held her in his arms, stroking her hair.

"Sometimes," she gasped. "Sometimes . . . I come home . . . And I just . . . sit here. And there's this kind of *tightness* in my chest. It's like I can't breathe! I am so sorry . . ."

"No," he said, cradling her in his arms. "Don't be sorry. It's okay. You don't have to be sorry."

The tears streamed down Alex's face. Dan

held her. He rocked her back and forth on the bathroom floor. "No," he said over and over. "You're all right. You don't have to be sorry."

After a while, he put her to bed. He picked up a pillow that had fallen to the floor. He found a blanket in her closet and covered her with it. She said she had prescription pain-killers in the medicine cabinet. Dan went back into the bathroom and got a couple for her.

As he closed the medicine chest door, he made the mistake of looking in the mirror, coming face-to-face with his own grim reflection. The man in the mirror was not the same man he'd seen after his shower this morning. That one had been glad to be home, eager to call Beth, looking forward to spending a quiet Sunday getting some work done. . . .

Dan had a chilling premonition he might never see that man again.

"You'll feel better when you get some sleep," he told Alex. He sat beside her on the bed, watching as she swallowed the pills. She lay back, looking very pale. All her defenses were down. She seemed totally vulnerable. "I'll stay here tonight," he said.

"You don't have to. I'm okay now."

"No," he said. "I want to."

She tried to smile.

"It's okay;" he said. "I'll be in the other room if you need me."

"Thank you for being so kind," Alex said tiredly.

He smoothed back her hair. "Go to sleep, okay?" He got up and switched off the bedside light. Alex turned over and curled up. She looked young and small alone in the bed.

Dan paced the loft for a while. Quincy followed at his heels. Absentmindedly he scratched and patted the dog. When he stopped at the phone in the entryway, Quincy settled down under a large potted palm nearby.

Dan dialed the Rogersons' number. Beth answered, and he spoke, keeping his voice low. He didn't want to disturb Alex, didn't want to be overheard by her.

"How are you?" he asked, trying to force some life into his voice. "Did you just call me?"

"No."

"Oh," he said, groping. "I was in the shower . . . and the phone rang. I thought maybe it was you."

"Nope," she said, suppressing a yawn.

Dan looked at his watch. It was remarkably early. It felt like one A.M. It was not even nine-thirty yet. "Well, how are you? Did you have a good day?"

"We went to see the house," she answered, reviving somewhat.

"Yeah? And . . ." Dan picked up the phone and walked with it to the door of Alex's bedroom. He stared in at her. He couldn't tell if she was asleep. Her eyes were closed, but he wasn't sure. He thought she might be listening.

Quietly he carried the phone back to the entryway, listening to Beth's excited description of the house. "Yeah, yeah . . ." he said, turning his back on Alex's door. "You know I'm not against it, don't get the wrong idea. It's just a question of the money."

"I know," she said, ever the good scout. "If we can't afford it, we can't afford it. What are you up to?"

He wanted to tell her. He wanted desperately to be able to talk to Beth. She was the only one he trusted completely. But he couldn't tell her. Dan felt sick with the sudden knowledge that the one person who could heal him was the one he couldn't share his pain with.

"Nothing much," he said tenderly. "I think I'll get a bite. Kick in early, go to bed. I'm wiped." He rubbed his eyes and was startled to discover he was crying.

"See you tomrrow," Beth said.

"Okay, darling. I love you."

"I love you, too," she said.

He didn't want to say good-bye. "Okay, well . . ." he said.

Beth said, "Good night, darling," and hung up.

After that, he looked in on Alex again. She was fast asleep now. Her steady breathing told him so. Dan wandered into the kitchen. The sink and counter were bloody. There were bloodstains on the floor. He found the knife she'd used to cut herself. He tossed it into the sink, rolled up his sleeves, and cleaned the place up.

Gallagher looked in on her again, then paced the living room. The cassette of *Madame Butterfly* was still in the tape deck. He thought about taking it out, putting it away. He reached for it, then hesitated, remembering the strange melancholy the music had stirred in him earlier, remembering the terror years ago. The huge dark opera house. The desperate woman on stage.

"What's the matter, Dad?" he'd asked the stern silhouette beside him. "Why is the lady so sad?"

"Because he's leaving her."

"But why, Daddy?"

"Shhhh," his father had said. "Just watch. She's going to kill herself."

"No!" Dan had blurted out. He'd put his hands over his ears and shouted, "No!"

"Dan," his father had whispered gruffly.

Dan had begun to cry then. Shame and terror had driven him under his seat. But the shame he'd felt for crying, for embarrassing his father, was nothing compared to the shame he'd felt because he wanted to save poor Butterfly and couldn't.

That shame, that terror, from which he'd hidden thirty-three years ago, had caught up with him tonight.

Gallagher left the cassette where it was. Exhausted, he sat down on the sofa. He tried to browse through the *Times* again, to occupy his mind. The lines between the past and present were blurring for him; his adult life and the nightmares of his childhood had suddenly become interchangeable. He leafed through the newspaper and, after a while, he fell asleep.

Sometime after midnight, he got up and went into the bedroom and lay down on top of the covers, fully dressed, beside Alex. And that was where he woke at dawn. He got up quietly and stepped over to the window. The meat markets below were in full swing.

Dan leaned over the bed. "Alex?" He stirred her gently.

She opened her eyes. It took her a second or two to focus on him. She smiled weakly.

"How are you feeling?" he asked.

"Okay."

"Does it hurt?"

She moved her wrists from side and side and winced. "A little," she said.

He nodded. "Yeah. I've got to go now, Alex."

"Will you call me sometime?" she said sleepily. "You don't have to if you don't want to."

"No, no. I will. If you promise me you'll see the doctor." He bent forward and kissed her on the forehead. "Good-bye," Dan said.

"Good-bye, Dan."

"You take care."

"You, too," Alex said.

Dan paused at the door and looked back at her. She turned over and went back to sleep.

He got home with the dog about five-thirty. He showered and shaved, pulled back the bedclothes, and ruffled the sheets until he was satisfied that the bed had a suitably slept-in look. He packed his briefcase and was halfway out the door when he remembered the spaghetti. He tore back into the kitchen and took the pan of spaghetti out of the refrigerator and gave it to Quincy, who cleaned it up and was sniffing around for more before Dan hit the front door again.

In the cab on the way to the office, it occurred to him that it was not just Beth he'd been trying to protect when he messed up the bed and fed the spaghetti to Quincy. Not just Beth and Ellen. It was his own ass, Dan realized, his own life, which was nothing without them.

He'd hardly made a dent in *Rogers* v. *Winitsky* when Martha peeked into his office.

"What are you doing here?" the secretary asked. "It's eight A.M."

Dan looked up from his work and hiked up the reading glasses that were sliding down his nose. "I'm in the shithouse, Martha," he told her. "I'm supposed to be in court by two and I'm really behind. Do me a favor, cancel everything, and call Drimmer—tell him we're fine and I'll see him there at two."

Martha raised her eyebrows and gave him a look. "At two," she repeated, backing out the door. "O-kay."

Dan took off his glasses and pinched the bridge of his nose. He looked like hell. He'd read it in Martha's look. But the sight of her, even of her admonishing glance, was disproportionately pleasing to him this morning. She looked perfectly ordinary—just his everyday forty-six-year-old cheerfully cynical secretary. Just Martha. But it felt awfully good this morning to be back to the grind, back to everyday life and everyday Martha. . . .

"Good morning, Martha," Dan called. The morning dragged. He had lunch at his desk and caught up on mail and calls, then he rushed over to the courts to meet Bob Drimmer. Henry was with him. "Sorry I couldn't make it on Saturday," he said to Dan. "I hope my new editor was helpful."

Dan nodded. He wondered where Alex was right now. She wouldn't have come in to work. She was probably still sleeping. He thought maybe he ought to call her tomorrow. Just to find out if she'd seen a doctor or gone to a hospital. Just to make sure she was all right.

He told himself he'd call her. Tomorrow. Maybe the next day.

He couldn't wait to get home.

It was dark out by the time Dan left the office. He was pretty wiped out. But the sound of his daughter's voice revived him as he took his key out of the door.

"Daddy!" Ellen charged down the hall and jumped into his arms before he had time to take off his coat.

"Hey," Dan said, laughing, "how's my main squeeze?" He kissed her chipmunk cheeks and, clutching her awkwardly in his arms, headed for the kitchen.

Ellen chattered nonstop as they made their way along the corridor. "We had a great time!" she declared, with wide-eyed breathlessness. "I went for a walk with Grandpa and we saw rabbits and Sally dog chased them but she didn't catch any and—"

"Whoa," Gallagher said. "Slow down, El. I can't understand a word you're saying."

Beth was waiting in the kitchen with a big

smile on her face. Ellen scrambled out of his arms. "But, Daddy, I want a rabbit. . . ." she was saying.

Dan felt his throat catch at the sight of Beth. He was very tired. He hadn't realized, until he saw her, how emotionally drained he was.

"Hi, darling," she said.

He felt as though he might cry. His throat was thick. He cleared it, and sighed. "Hi, babe," he said softly. "I really missed you."

Ellen tugged at the handle of his briefcase. She had made it her job, just a few months ago, to take it to the desk when he came home. Dan gave it to her and, with a proud effort, she carried it off.

"Liar," Beth chided him.

"I did," he said, taking her into his arms. He kissed her tenderly and, feeling tears begin to well in him, buried his face in her hair and held her tight. "I missed you a lot," he said. The sweet, clean smell of her shampoo and her talcumed neck were balm to him. Dan laughed like an overtired kid and kissed her again.

"Hey," Beth said, grinning with surprise and delight. "I should go away more often."

After dinner, as Beth cleared the table, Ellen showed her father a new card trick she'd learned. Dan sat on the floor across the coffee table from her and shook his head admiringly at the sight of her tiny hands struggling to shuffle the grown-up-size deck.

He was crazy about those perfect little hands, those fragile, sticky fingertips, and, at the moment, chocolate-rimmed nails. He remembered how awesome the first sight of those hands had been to him, the tiny fists he'd freed from their protective flannel sleeve mitts, the fists in which a pebble would have seemed a boulder.

"Now pick a card," Ellen said, presenting the deck to him.

Beth strolled into the living room and put her hands on Dan's shoulder.

"Any card?" he asked Ellen.

Her brow furrowed, her tongue poked out in concentration. She glanced up at her mother, who nodded.

"Yes," Ellen said, relieved.

Dan picked a card as Beth went back to clearing the table. "Where'd she learn this?" he asked her.

"Grandpa showed me!" Ellen said, " 'Course, Grandma is too old."

With great absorption, and much to Dan's delight, she began to deal the cards into rows.

"Do I show it to you?" he asked her.

"No." She was the expert now. A very definite no. "You put it back."

"It's one of those long tricks . . . I can tell," Dan said. "My favorite kind," he reassured Ellen. To Beth, he asked, "So . . . how was it?"

She was on her way back to the kitchen with a pile of dishes. "How was what?" she called over her shoulder.

"Come on. I'm a big boy. I can take it."

Ellen leaned all the way across the table to tell him in his ear. Dan leaned forward to listen. "It has a place for rabbits," his daughter confided.

Dan made a terrible face. "Oh, no! Yuck," he said.

Beth returned with two coffee mugs and sat down beside him. The sight of him clutching his throat and making guttural sounds did not, apparently, strike her as anything out of the ordinary.

"She said it," Dan ranted, with a dying gasp. "She said the R word."

"What can I tell you?" Beth said calmly. "It's perfect."

"Daddy! Is it in this row?"

In his death throes, Dan squinted at her. He lifted one eye and peeked at the cards on the table. "No," he said.

"So . . . when are you going to come up and take a look," Beth asked offhandedly. "Just for the hell of it?"

"Is this the row?" Ellen pointed.

"No," Dan told her. "How about first thing in the morning?" he said to Beth.

"Dan!" she said, surprised and very excited.

"Daddy. Which row?"

"This one, sweetheart," Dan said, looking over his shoulder at Beth.

"You mean it?" She could hardly contain herself.

"Yeah," he said, grinning. "I mean it—if you can get me back to town by one o'clock."

He was happy to be home, to be with them again.

"Wait, that's wrong, I made a mistake." Ellen groaned in exasperation. "Oh, phooey. Now I have to start all over!" She gathered up the cards.

And Dan grinned and thought it was fine. It was fine with him if it took all night.

—— 6 ——

Tuesday morning dawned clear and crisp. They dropped Ellen off at school and drove up the Saw Mill Parkway to Westchester. Spears of sunlight shot between the trees lining the road. It was early autumn, and the leaves had not yet begun to turn.

Dan felt swept away by the benevolent weather and the irresistible appeal of autumn in the country. In Manhattan, he side-skirted street trash endlessly. Now, suddenly, a balled-up newspaper blowing across the highway offended him. He had become a manor lord less than an hour out of the city.

When they got to Mt. Kisco, the real estate agent poured them two Styrofoam cups full of fresh-brewed coffee. She offered to drive them to the house in her Mazda, but they elected to take their own car. In the silver Volvo, they followed her along sunswept country lanes and tree-lined roads. And Dan felt himself falling for it—the soft rolling land, the well-tended homes terraced with mossy stone walls, birch trees, and thick pines.

"There it is," Beth said. "It needs a bit of work, of course. . . ."

Dan looked up and saw a small two-story timber house, the white paint somewhat flaked. Appended to it, an old-fashioned front porch and a two-car garage. By itself, unimpressive. But sitting there, at the rise of a gentle sloping hill, it commanded a spectacular view of the open countryside. It had, Dan thought as he tried to suppress a grin, dream house potential.

Beth took his hand and dragged him inside. Their footsteps echoed on the bare floorboards of the empty house. Light streamed in through the wide windows. Dan looked around, impressed.

"Well?" Beth asked, sensing victory.

Bea Murdoch, the real estate agent was waiting in the front hall. She beamed at Dan. He winked at her. "It's okay," he said to Beth, stifling his enthusiasm.

"Okay? What do you mean, 'okay'!" He hadn't fooled her. "It's fantastic," she prompted.

"Shhhh," he cautioned, leading her away from Mrs. Murdoch toward the substantial old kitchen with its pantry and spacious cupboards. "Fantastic," he agreed, slipping his arm around her waist. "It's great, just great."

"Just think of all the money we'll save by not living in New York," she said excitedly. "And I can get a job teaching, once I get my certificate."

"Right," Dan said dubiously. "Oh, yeah."

"No, it's true." She led him through the kitchen into the dining room with its brick fireplace and wainscoting and notched oak floor. They continued on to the airy living room.

"The local high school's excellent," Bea Murdoch called. "My own children went there."

"You see?" Beth said, squeezing him affectionately.

"This really is a terrific area for kids," the agent continued.

"Yes, I'm sure," Dan said. They were back at the entrance hall. "Would it be okay," he asked, pointing to the stairs, "if we . . . ?"

"Oh, please. Go right ahead," she said, "I'll wait for you down here."

Beth led him upstairs, pointing out railings, baseboards, ceiling fixtures, and other mundane features as if she were a tour guide at the Sistine Chapel. In her excitement, she sounded like Ellen, Dan thought. She looked like Ellen, too. All lit up with enthusiasm and possibility.

He followed her from room to room, his resistance weakening, his objections sounding less and less convincing, trying to be intelligent, reserved, trying not to look like what he was, already converted, a rubbernecking, awestruck pilgrim.

"We'd still have to decorate," he temporized.

"There's nothing we can't fix ourselves. We can have painting parties."

"*Painting parties?*" He grinned and shook his head at her. "Beth, you're making me very nervous."

She kissed him lightly on the lips, then spun around. "Look at this," she said, rushing off again. "A trapdoor!" And she pulled down a set of steps that led up to an attic room.

That did it. He was a boy again. He took her hand and pulled her up the shallow flight with him into a large, sunny room. "Wow! Look at this!" Dan laughed. "This is fantastic! This is great!"

They walked across the varnished wood floor and peered out the two windows cut into the sloping roof. The ceiling had been plastered over between beams, leaving the lovely old wood exposed. It was a really skillful conversion.

"Wouldn't it make a terrific playroom?" Beth said.

Dan stopped pretending. He was utterly won over. "What are you talking about, playroom? This is my den!"

"Oh!" she said, giving her little excited jump, instinctively clapping her hands. "I knew you'd like it!" She wrapped her arms around him.

"How about making it a nursery?" He leered. He squeezed her tightly to him and waggled his eyebrows. Then he gave her a big kiss and pushed her back toward the floor, pretending to ravish her.

Beth resisted laughingly. "I already did that." She giggled. "Dan, stop it . . ."

She managed to trip him. They fell together to the floor as she laughed and kissed him back. And, suddenly, they were moving against one another, grinning mouth to mouth, and breathing hard. "Why don't we christen this little sucker right here?" Dan whispered against her ear.

"Are you all right up there?"

Beth buried her face in his shoulder to stifle her laughter.

"Yes, thank you," Dan called down to Mrs.

Murdoch. "We're fine . . . aren't we?" he asked Beth.

They were back in the city by one. Beth dropped him off at the office. She was double-parked in heavy traffic. He leaned back into the car to kiss her and set off a cacophony of horns, hoots, and impatient catcalls.

"Later," Dan capitulated. Waving at her, he hurried into the building. On the elevator, he caught himself staring at an extremely attractive girl, then caught himself. He looked down at the wall, then at his feet, and finally at a baby in a stroller, who watched him for a moment with what seemed to Dan, a knowing look.

He was in a great mood. He got off the elevator and started down the hall at a good clip. "Hi, Eunice," he said to the receptionist. She handed him a sheaf of phone messages. "Martha back from lunch yet?" he asked, flipping through them.

"She just got back."

He smiled and looked up at her. She nodded beyond him to the waiting area, and he followed her glance. Alex Forrest was sitting there.

Dan felt as though he'd been punched in the gut. With effort, he hung on to his ebbing smile.

"Hi," she said softly.

"Hello," he said, then looked over his shoulder at Eunice, who was watching them with curiosity. Something in his look made the receptionist turn away. He guessed he wasn't pulling off his casual act.

Alex looked somewhat severe in a well-cut dark suit, and far more beautiful than he remembered.

He didn't want to remember.

She seemed ill at ease. For some reason, that made him feel a little bit better.

"I hope this isn't inconvenient. I was in the area. . . ." she began.

Before she finished, he'd started shaking his head, no, no inconvenience, of course not. His head was on automatic, with his smile and his casual air.

"I figured . . ." Alex continued, and then she trailed off.

"No, no," Dan said. "Would you like to come into my office?"

They walked along in silence, both of them smiling tightly, nervously.

"Hey! Dan!" Jimmy Lawrence called to him as they passed the open door of his office. He was pacing in his carpeted cell, dictating to Molly, his secretary. He had a rubber band around his wrist and was toying with it mindlessly.

Dan stopped automatically and looked in on him. Alex paused as well.

"Will you be in your office later?" Jimmy asked. "There's something I need to go over with you."

"Sure," Dan said.

Jimmy was studying Alex curiously. He seemed momentarily perplexed. "Don't I know you?" he asked, making a slingshot of the rubberband. "Haven't we met somewhere?"

"I can't imagine," Alex said coolly, and continued walking.

"Brrr," Jimmy said, lifting his collar, as Dan hurried off. "She's wild for me," he confided to Molly. "She's just trying to be cool so Gallagher doesn't get all bent out of shape."

"Yeah, right," Dan heard Molly say as he continued along the corridor to his office.

Martha looked up from her desk. Dan gave her a smile and ushered Alex past her, into his office. He could feel Martha's eyes boring a hole into his back. He glanced over his shoulder and, sure enough, she was staring at him with a little intrigued smile on her face and her head cocked to one side, as if she'd asked him a question and was waiting for an answer.

Dan closed the door on her.

Automatically he crossed the room to his desk and sat in his leather swivel chair. He motioned Alex to the chair in front of the desk. "Have a seat," he said, uneasy with the strained formality.

"Thanks." She smiled again, the same pinched smile. She was as uncomfortable as he. She looked down at her lap, at her hands, which were fidgeting with her gloves, and he couldn't help glancing at her wrists. But they were covered by the long sleeves of her black jacket.

"Are you okay?" Dan asked. "I was going to call you today. . . ."

"I'm fine," Alex said. She hadn't actually looked up. She'd only stolen a sidelong glance at him. "Listen . . ." she continued. "I find this terribly embarrassing. . . . I just wanted to say 'sorry' for what happened. I had no right to put you through all that."

He was shaking his head reassuringly, again. "Nothing happened," he said. "Okay?" But he was relieved that she'd brought it up, gotten it out in the open. He was relieved that she sounded sane again. He felt himself begin to relax.

Alex smiled gratefully. "The fact is," she continued, determined, it seemed, to explain herself, "I'd been going through a bad time. I was coming to some sort of crisis. I feel much better now. . . ." Her smile shifted gears from repentant to cautiously confident, he noticed.

It put him more at ease. "Thanks to you," she said. She lowered her eyes modestly for a moment. Then her thick eyelashes swept up again, and her pale green eyes caught his. "So . . . thank you."

Dan held her gaze, then laughed and turned his attention to pushing a pencil back and forth on his desk. "You don't have to thank me."

Alex waited until he looked up at her again. "Oh yes, I do," she insisted, with a toss of her head. She brushed back her hair. It was a confident gesture. She was clearly more comfortable now. She was looking directly at him. There wasn't much humility left in her smile.

"Most guys would have just taken off. Run away. I don't know what might have happened . . . what I would have done if you hadn't been there."

Dan accepted her gratitude with a gracious nod. After a beat, he said, "You're looking good."

She returned the nod.

"As a matter of fact, you look great." He was warming to her. Now that she sounded okay, normal, healthy again, it was easy to see what he'd found attractive in her. She was beautiful, bright, sexy, and strong. Strong had been one of the things that had attracted him to begin with.

"Thanks," Alex said quietly.

There was a moment's silence. Dan wasn't sure what was coming next, what was expected of him.

"So . . ." she said, at last. "All that's in the past."

He nodded. He smiled.

"I was wondering . . . would you do me . . ." she laughed. "Well, I'd like to ask one more favor."

Dan shifted awkwardly in his chair. "What's that?"

"I've got tickets for *Madame Butterfly* two weeks from Thursday—"

"No," he began, shaking his head.

"It's the twenty-fourth. I'd be very grateful if you'd let me take you. A peace offering."

"It's very kind of you," he continued, "really. But I really don't think it's a good idea."

He was very clear now. It was over. However bright and strong she was, however sexy and beautiful, it was over. Nothing was worth the terror he'd gone through this weekend. Nothing was worth losing his family over. They were going to get the house. They were going to leave the city. It was an omen. A new start. He'd screwed up and gotten away with it by the skin of his teeth and it had taught him a lesson he must have needed to learn— because he was very, very clear now.

"No strings attached," Alex said. She was smiling at him, one of those vulnerable, brave smiles.

"No," he said, and then he thought, Well, there was no reason to be cruel. "Alex, under different circumstances . . ." he began gently.

"You don't have to explain. I just thought I'd ask." She stood up. "Well . . ." The quavering smile again, but brave. "I'll see you sometime." She held out her hand.

"Sure," he said, and went to shake hands, and then he thought about her wrists, and thought, for Chrissake, Gallagher, you slept with this woman. "Hey," he said gently, opening his arms to her, like a friend, a pal, a generous guy.

They kissed.

"So long. Take care," he said.

Alex nodded understandingly. "Good-bye."

He escorted her to the door and closed it after her. And then he shook his head and let out a deep breath.

The next few weeks were among the busiest Dan could remember. Things were hopping at work and twice as wild at home. They were buying the house, for a start. And that entailed endless phone calls and trips to the bank, days of doing and nights of planning . . . and lists . . . pages and pages of lists.

There wasn't time to think of Alex Forrest. Then, one night when he and Beth went out bowling with Jimmy and Hildy, she entered his thoughts.

None of them could bowl. It was a harebrained idea, but they'd gone to dinner in the neighborhood and afterward, instead of standing on line for the movies, Jimmy suggested bowling. For some reason, the girls were wild to try it.

When Dan tried to dismiss the idea, Beth and Hildy had jumped all over him. They'd gone so far as to boo him when he stood up and excused himself to go to the men's room. He'd played the bad guy for a little while. Mainly because they were having such a good time putting him down. Then he graciously gave in and became their hero.

The lanes were on the second floor of an old brick warehouse building on Amsterdam Avenue. Hildy's baby-sitter had told them about it, told them that it used to be a teenage hangout until the Yuppies moved into the neighborhood. Now it was just another endangered West Side landmark in the throes of gentrification.

It didn't look all that endangered, Dan thought. At one end of the slightly seedy alley, there was a genuine fifties Formica bar packed with cigarette burns. Six venerable aluminum stools, crowned with marbleized red plastic seats, stood in front of it, and dusty bags of potato chips hung from a metal rack next to the cash register.

Beautiful, it wasn't. But busy. Packed to the max. The lanes were filled with a cross section of the neighborhood. Leather-jacketed teens kibbitzed trendy college kids, Hispanic families sent their children for more beer and chips, a hard-drinking tattooed couple took time out between shots to rock the sleeping baby in the stroller next to their scoring table. Ther were even middle-aged lawyers in the place. A team of them, two of whom Jimmy and Dan recognized from their baseball league.

They rented shoes and sat on the red marbleized seats, laughing and drinking beer until their number was called. They were uniformly terrible at the game.

Then, when it was his turn to keep score, Dan noticed the date Hildy had scrawled onto the corner of their scorecard. The twenty-fourth. It touched off something. He tried to recall what it was about the date. . . . He remembered it was the night Alex had tickets for *Madame Butterfly*.

That was it. It was no big deal.

Jimmy hollered for him to drag his butt back onto the alley. And Dan did. He got up and took the ball Jimmy handed him. And he shuddered suddenly.

"What's up, baby? Cold feet?" Jimmy teased.

It was Alex. He'd seen her in his mind. Clearly. She was all alone. She was elegantly dressed and sitting alone at the opera. It was the beginning of Act II. Butterfly was singing of her love for Pinkerton and her dreams of his return "one fine day". . . .

"Dan?"

He saw her. Her green eyes were cold. She sat impassively, devoid of emotion.

"Hey, hey, hey," Jimmy called. "Let's go, Ralphie!"

"Come on, honey," Beth was cheering him on. "We need a strike."

"Yeah, one for the Gipper!" Hildy called.

Dan looked at them. Their joy, their boisterousness and good-natured liveliness were balm to him. He bowled one for them. And damned if he didn't get a strike.

—— 7 ——

From the moment of his vision at the bowling alley (if that's what it had been), Dan had a feeling he'd be hearing from Alex soon. He was on the money. She phoned him at the office at ten the next morning. He got the message at 10:45 and told Martha he'd call back later.

It was a busy morning and he forgot about it. When he came back from lunch at two-thirty, Martha handed him two piles of yellow message slips. The first group were business calls. The second were Alex's. She had phoned him about every fifteen minutes since ten-thirty.

"Didn't you tell her I'd call back?" Dan asked, knowing that, of course, Martha had.

His normally unflappable secretary gave him an evil look as she nodded.

"Okay," he said. "Sorry. Okay, I'll call her right now."

"Thank you," Martha said.

Dan didn't even take his coat off before he dialed Robbins and Hart. "Alex Forrest," he said, standing at his desk.

"Alex?" he said when she picked up.

"Dan? How good to hear your voice." She was calm, unhurried. There was no emergency.

"You called me. Is something wrong?"

"I saw our favorite opera last night. No, of course there's nothing wrong. It was glorious, Dan. I . . . I'm sorry you couldn't make it. It was—"

"Alex," he cut her off. "I thought there was something the matter, some emergency. Martha tells me you've been calling all morning. Didn't she tell you I'd call back when I got a chance?"

"Oh," she said, "I'm sorry. I was on the phone most of the morning. I wasn't sure whether you'd tried and just didn't get through—"

"Alex. This doesn't work—"

"What's that?" she asked earnestly.

"This," he said, transferring the telephone receiver from hand to hand as he pulled off his coat. "Your calling. I'm busy, Alex. I've been very busy and, well, I just don't think it's a good idea. We talked about it, didn't we?"

"Yes. I thought it was all right. I thought we'd agreed that just once in a while . . . Didn't we say, maybe we'd see each other sometime?"

"I don't know. I don't remember. But I think it's best now if we don't."

"Of course." She sounded wounded. "I understand." Her voice was thick: Jesus, Dan thought, she can't be crying.

"You're all right, aren't you? You're feeling okay, and everything? I mean, there's nothing . . ."

Martha poked her head in the door. She tapped her watch with a pencil, signaling him that his two-thirty meeting was about to begin. He held his hand up and nodded. "Right there," he mouthed.

"Alex, I'm awfully sorry. Honest. I've got to go now. I've got a meeting starting. Thanks for calling. I hope you're feeling better. I mean, I'm glad you enjoyed the opera." He didn't know what the hell he was saying.

"Dan. I was hoping that maybe . . ."

"No," he said, too sharply. "Listen, I'm sorry. Really I am."

"You keep apologizing."

He laughed. "Yeah. Well. I do, don't I?"

"You don't have to. Don't you think I understand?"

"I hope so, Alex. I really do. Listen, I've got to go now. Good-bye," he said, and hung up.

He stood there for a minute looking down at the phone. It was almost as if he expected it to ring again. He stood, watching it, waiting.

Then, "Jesus!" he said aloud, and crumpled the yellow phone messages into a ball and shot them through the basketball-hoop attachment Beth had bought him for his wastebasket. Swish. Two points. He'd gotten lucky.

Two weeks later, as Gallagher was leaving Jimmy's office, Arthur Ashley caught up to him.

"About *Rogers* v. *Watchamacallit*," the tall and dapper partner said, overtaking Dan.

"Winitsky."

"Right," Arthur snapped, picking up the pace just enough to make the younger man work to keep up with him. "I got your memo. You're going to go for summary judgment?"

"Why not?" Dan moved briskly alongside Arthur, ticking points off on his fingertips. "The facts aren't in dispute. Rogers admits he read Winitsky's article. The only question is, did he plagiarize it in his book?"

Arthur nodded judiciously. "Yes, yes, I see."

"As we know, you can't copyright an *idea*, just the *expression* of an idea. Rogers certainly didn't use any of the *words* in the book."

"Let me think about it, okay?"

"Sure," Dan said.

The tall man put an avuncular hand on Dan's shoulder. "So, I hear you're about to become a suburbanite."

"Yeah, we took the plunge."

Arthur smiled approvingly, "Got a buyer for the apartment?"

"Not yet." Dan strode briskly alongside him.

"Got cold sweats about your escrow?"

"Maybe a little . . ."

Arthur stopped short at the door to Dan's outer office. "But not about Rogers and Winitsky?"

"No, sir," Dan said.

Arthur eyed him shrewdly, appraisingly.

Dan heard Martha's voice. She was on the phone, and she sounded unusually cold.

"He's still in a meeting. . . . Yes, I know, I did expect him to be through by now." She was all forced patience and formality.

He gave her a questioning glance. She rolled her eyes in exasperation.

Arthur had apparently made a decision. He clapped a hand on Dan's shoulder again. "I'd like you to have lunch with me on Tuesday, if you're around," he said.

"That would be great, Arthur. Thank you. It'll be my pleasure. Let me just check my diary." He hurried to the desk.

"You *are* on his list of calls," Martha was saying. She put her hand over the receiver. "It's Alex Forrest," she told him.

He frowned. "Again? I thought you told her I'd call back." Dan couldn't help glancing over his shoulder to where Arthur was still hovering in the doorway.

"I did," Martha said. "Twice in the past hour."

"Let me see the diary. Put her on hold."

He turned the pages as he walked back to Arthur. Behind him he heard, "Would you mind holding? He'll be free in a moment."

"Arthur," Dan said. "Tuesday'd be great, Arthur. Thank you." He waited until Arthur had turned the corner, then he hurried into his office. "Put her through," he said.

He picked up the phone. "Hello? Look, Alex," he said with barely restrained anger. "I thought we'd agreed this wasn't a good idea."

"I have to see you," she said.

"Why? What for?"

"There's something we have to discuss," Alex said.

"I'm sorry. I thought you understood." He

tried to be reasonable, straining to keep his voice normal, even friendly now. "If I've some-how given you the wrong idea, I apologize. But I think it's best if we don't talk to each other anymore."

He hung up and signaled Martha on the intercom. "If she calls again, tell her I'm out," he said.

She was sitting in front of the mirror in her bra and panties, putting on her lipstick. Her curly hair was caught up in a ponytail to keep it out of her face while she got ready. Springy sun-bleached tendrils of hair escaped onto the nape of her neck.

Dan walked in from the bathroom and watched her for a while. Then he came up behind her, put his arms around her, and kissed her neck. "Mmmmm, you smell good," he said.

"Mmmm, you kiss good," Beth responded.

He moved his lips from the nape of her neck to her shoulder and then started kiss-ing down toward her breasts, which were cupped in her low-cut apricot silk bra.

"Dan," she said gently, "they're going to be here in a minute."

He kissed her on the lips and she responded, her lips parting for him. When she broke away, he looked at her in the mirror. "God, you're beautiful."

Beth seemed surprised and touched by his feeling, a little awed by its intensity, but clearly pleased. She reached up to stroke his cheek and Gallagher began kissing her again. The doorbell stopped him.

"Wouldn't you know?" Beth said, smiling.

Jimmy and Hildy swept in with laughter and gifts. In addition to dessert, they'd brought a couple of bottles of Dom Perignon.

They were all seated around the dining-room table when Jimmy pried the cork off one of the bottles with a loud pop. They cheered excitedly as frothing champagne spilled over the table. Dan lit up the cigar Hildy had brought him.

"Ladies and gentlemen," Jimmy announced. "My wife . . . my ball and chain . . . mother of some of my children . . ."

Hildy poked him. "You should have such a ball and chain."

"A toast," Jimmy continued. "Here's to Miller, Goodman, Hurst . . . and Gallagher!"

There were raucous cheers all around. "Here, here!" Hildy shouted, tapping her water glass with a spoon.

"Guys," Dan protested, "all he did was ask me to lunch."

"—and they're moving to their country estate. They'll forget they ever knew us plebs."

"Now wait a minute," Dan said without

cracking a smile. "I want you to know I've been reading one of those self-help books lately—"

"Published by Robbins and Hart, of course!"

"Of course." Dan bowed to Jimmy." *Samurai Self-Help*. And it tells how to deal with the anxieties of friends as you move up the corporate ladder . . . and they stay put, or, God forbid, move down. . . ."

Hildy hissed. Beth said, "Oh, Dan!" and got up to get the strawberries.

Jimmy looked over his beefy shoulder, smoothed back his thinning hair, then squinted at Dan. "You talkin' to *me*?" he challenged. "To *me*? Well, there's no one else here—"

Hildy shook her head. "He's been trying to get DeNiro for ten years. It's pathetic," she confided to Dan. "A sad thing."

"Moving right along," Dan said, straightfaced again. "And in this book it tells you not to coddle the anxieties of those friends. So I'm not going to make a lot of false reassurances." He waved his cigar, flicked the ashes grandly. "I can't say you'll be up every weekend. Let's face it, things have changed."

Hildy booed him.

Dan shrugged. "This isn't a classless society. As a matter of fact, this is good-bye, guys!"

"Dan . . ." Beth returned from the kitchen.

"Well, honey, it's best to make a clean break. We're on our way, we want to travel light. . . ."

The telephone rang. She put the bowl of strawberries onto the table and went into the living room to answer it.

"—and then, of course," Dan continued. "Not everyone belongs in Westchester."

He heard her say, "Hello? Hello?" and looked over at her. Alex, his sixth sense told him.

Beth hung up with a frown and returned to the table. "Nobody there. That's the second time tonight," she said.

Dan's smile vanished. "The second time?"

She nodded. "I hate that. It gives me the creeps."

Hildy shuddered. "Me, too. I'm always afraid it's someone trying to case the joint."

"Oh, no, don't worry," Jimmy said. "It's probably just one of Dan's girlfriends."

They all laughed. Only Dan was caught off guard by the jibe. "Yeah," he said, after a beat, "but which one?"

He had a hard time getting to sleep that night. He didn't actually fall off until after one. The phone jarred him awake again. Instinctively he reached for it before it could ring a second time. Beth stirred drowsily in her sleep.

"Yeah?" he said.

"At last." Alex's voice was vengeful and cold.

Dan shot an anxious glance in Beth's direction. She was slowly waking up.

"Oh?" Dan said. "Richard. It's kind of late, isn't it?"

"If you keep refusing my calls at the office, you leave me no choice."

"Look, it's two in the morning here," he said. "Can't this wait till tomorrow morning?"

"Oh," Alex said with a cool chuckle. "Is it *inconvenient*? Is it awkward for you to talk?"

"You could say that."

Intrigued by a call at that late hour, Beth glanced at him through sleep-squinty eyes. He shrugged at her and shook his head, sharing her upset. Her gaze went from curious to sympathetic. She closed her eyes again.

"I've got to see you," Alex said.

"I . . . I don't have the . . . the documentation here to answer that question. I'll call you from the office, okay?"

"No," she snapped. "Meet me in front of the Robbins and Hart building at six."

He didn't want to see her again. He looked over at Beth. He was going to have to tell her. If the calls kept up, he'd have to do it. Shit, Dan thought. How could he have done this, screwed up this way? She'd probably forgive him. In time. But it would hurt her. And that hurt might be irreparable.

"Listen . . . Richard. Let me just think about that—"

"Don't disappoint me," Alex said ominously.

He gave in. "You can rely on that," he said.

"Be there."

He hung up. Beth's eyes sprang open again. She was wide-awake now. "Who in the hell was that?" she asked, watching him with open curiosity.

"A client," Dan said, reaching for his cigarettes. "Jesus," he barked, turning away from her steady gaze. "These guys think they own you!"

"In the middle of the night?"

Now, he thought. Sit up. Put on the light. Tell her now.

"It's only eleven in L.A.," he said.

She turned over, turned her back on him. "Even so . . ." she said, disgruntled. She shifted around, trying to find a comfortable position. Finally she settled down. Dan remained on his back, wide-awake, long after he'd put out his second cigarette.

— 8 —

Dan tried not to think about it, but his whole day turned to shit. He couldn't concentrate in court. The best he could do was ask for a postponement, and the judge's annoyance was minor compared to Fred Kunstler's disgust. Kunstler was Robbins and Hart's hot new in-house counsel and he was eager to make his bones on the dispute raging between the publishing house and the Northern California Booksellers Association.

Dan was grateful that it wasn't Drimmer he was dealing with on this one. Or Henry Noonan, for that matter. Both of them would have been far more aware than Kunstler that Dan Gallagher was behaving oddly.

He got to the bank late, too, and had to make lame excuses to Beth. By way of apology, he took her to lunch and was preoccupied and snappish through most of it.

As he was packing his briefcase, Jimmy strolled into the office. "Half a day?" he teased, looking at his watch. Dan gave him a withering look and the big guy backed out on tiptoes. "Right," he said. "Next time, I bring the large corned beef, a whip, and a chair."

Dan couldn't find a cab. He took the subway uptown and arrived at the Robbins and Hart building a few minutes after six. Alex must have been waiting in the lobby. As he headed toward the building, she walked out alone. She started to take his arm.

"Don't," he said. "Please."

She was very calm. "All right," she agreed, walking west toward Sixth Avenue.

He waited until they were a couple of blocks from the publishing house. Then he said, "This has got to stop."

"What's that?" she asked.

"The phone calls, Alex!"

"Dan, if you'd agreed to see me, I wouldn't have had to call you."

"It hasn't registered, has it? It's over. There's nothing between us."

She glared at him, but her voice was chillingly even. "You mean you've had your fun, now you just want a quiet life."

He pulled her roughly into a doorway. "Alex, why are you doing this?" he demanded.

"Doing what?" she shot back scornfully.

Dan exploded. "You need help!" he shouted. He moved away. He thrust his hands deep into his coat pockets, to keep from slamming them into a wall. Alex hurried to catch up with him.

"You need a shrink!" he shouted at her. "A fucking doctor!"

People were looking at him, at them. Abashed, he turned left into the subway entrance near Radio City Music Hall. She followed him. He walked briskly through the endless corridors under Rockefeller Center.

"Why are you so hostile?" she asked, keeping up with him. "It really isn't necessary, you know. I'm not your enemy."

Dan was tired. "Then why are you trying to hurt me?" he said.

"Dan, don't," she said. She touched his arm. "I don't want to hurt you, Dan. I love you."

He stopped and spun to face her. "You what?"

She held his gaze and responded quietly, "I love you."

"You don't even know me."

"How can you say that?" she asked intensely.

He was baffled. "We spent the weekend together, Alex. That's it. That's as far as it goes."

"No," she said. "You stayed that second night. You must have liked me a little?"

"I was worried about you. Why do you have to read so much into everything?"

She winced, then looked down at her hands for a moment. And, suddenly, Gallagher realized that she really did believe that he felt something for her. Or that he ought to.

"Alex," he said as gently as he could, "can't you understand? I've got a whole life going with someone else. A very happy one."

"Whole means complete." Her shell of vulnerability cracked, revealing a brittle bitterness. "If your life's so damn complete, what were you doing with me?"

It was like a slap across the face. It brought him back to his senses, back to his anger. "Is this why you had to see me?" Dan demanded. "Is that what you want to talk about? Our imaginary love affair?"

"I'm pregnant," she said.

His jaw dropped.

"Now tell me you don't believe me." She was staring at him coolly.

"I don't believe you," he said.

Alex sighed and began rummaging in her purse. "I saw my gynecologist on Monday. Here." She handed him a card. Stunned, he accepted it without looking at it. "Here's his number if you want to call him," she said. "You can call him. . . ."

"Don't you—" he began.

"Use anything?" she finished the sentence for him. "No, I don't. I had a very bad miscarriage last year. I didn't think I *could* get pregnant."

He stared blindly at the card in his hand. "Are you sure . . . you're sure it's mine? How do you know it's mine?"

"Because," she said, controlling herself, "I don't sleep around."

Dan put the card in his pocket and took a deep breath. "Okay," he said, retrenching. "All right. I'm sorry. I apologize. Now, don't worry. I'm not going to let you handle this on your own."

"Handle what?" she asked with chilling openness.

"Well—the abortion. You don't have to worry about the money. I'll take care of it."

Alex smiled lovingly and shook her head at him. "What makes you think I'm going to have an abortion?"

Without realizing what he was doing, he took a step back. "No . . . no!" he said. "You're not going to have the baby!"

"Why not? There are plenty of successful one-parent families. At least," she said, smiling, "they don't end in divorce."

"Do I have any say in all this?"

She began to walk. Now, he was compelled to follow her.

"I want the child," Alex said firmly. "It has nothing to do with you. I'm going to have it, whether you want to be a part of it or not."

"Then why the hell are you telling me? Why not just do it?"

She turned to him with a subdued smile. "I was hoping you *would* want to be a part of it."

Dan shook his head in despair. "This is crazy, insane," he said. "This is just crazy!"

"I'm thirty-six years old. This may be my last chance to have a child—"

"Alex," he cut in. "For God's sake, think what you're saying. This is going to affect both of our lives forever!"

"Do you think I don't know that?" she asked earnestly. "I've thought about it a lot! I understand how you feel. It's a big thing, but it doesn't have to be a problem. Really, it doesn't . . . Play fair with me and I'll play fair with you, Dan."

She took his hand and placed her own over it reassuringly.

That night he sat at his desk in the living room while Beth read to Ellen. His wife and child were side by side at the dining table, looking at an *Oink and Pearl* book. From across the room, he could see Ellen's shiny scrubbed face. He could see her brow furrowed in concentration and her lips moving, trying to sound out the words her mother was reading aloud.

" 'Agnes and Nellie and Oink giggled and laughed in the dark,' " Beth read. "Who's this, Elle?" She pointed to a word in the book.

"Pearl!" Ellen announced. Then she glanced at her father to see if he'd witnessed her triumph.

Dan couldn't speak. He couldn't even smile. He winked at her. And Ellen, awkwardly, but full of pluck, tried to wink back. The gesture moved him nearly to tears.

He could not concentrate on his work. He could not take his eyes off them.

"Pearl, that's right. 'Pearl listened outside the door,' " Beth continued. " ' "Ooooo, it works," cried Nellie. "Of course," said Oink. "Look at the flying" . . .' "

"Dog!" Ellen shouted.

Beth laughed. "Yes! ' "Look at the flying dog," yelled Agnes. "Wow!" cried Nellie . . .' "

Sensing a presence, Beth looked up. She saw him staring at her. She smiled and went back to her reading. And Dan's throat filled with tears. Never had his family seemed more precious to him. As if he were afraid for them, as if it were his job to stand guard over them tonight, he dared not tear his eyes away.

Dan left for the office early the next morning, fully intending to put in a couple hours of work before the phones started ringing. He had a lot to catch up on. But when the train pulled into the Fourteenth Street Station, he got out.

He was about six long crosstown blocks from Alex's loft. He started to flag a cab, then glanced at his watch and figured he could make it walking.

He could have made it crawling. It was two hours before she left her building. The area was bustling. Beef carcases hung from the wooden eaves of archaic, low buildings. Refrigerated trucks crammed the cobbled streets. At every corner, gangs in butchers' coats, woolen hats, and gloves from which the fingers had been cut, warmed their hands over oil-drum fires. Dan waited across the street, watching the entrance to Alex's loft from a diner frequented by workers in bloody aprons.

Alex came out dressed for work. She walked past the men, ignoring their looks and catcalls, and turned the corner on her way to the subway.

Dan's heart started to pound. He gave her time to change her mind, to remember that she'd left something at home or discover a run in her stocking and return. When he was satisfied that she was out of the way, he raced across the street to her front door.

Impulsively he pressed all the buzzers. He was stressed out, breathing hard, jumpy as hell. After a moment, tenants began answering on the intercom. Finally someone buzzed. Dan rushed inside. Instead of taking the elevator, he raced up the stairs. At Alex's floor, he looked around then reached hastily for the key on top of the gas meter. It was there. He let himself into her apartment.

He hurried through the place, looking around. He didn't even know what the hell he was looking for—anything that would buy a little leverage, a little breathing space.

In the bathroom, he opened her medicine chest and stared dumbly at her many pills, the rows and rows of prescription medications. He pulled out his pocket diary and began to list the names of the pills in it. Two, he recognized as antidepressants, the same ones his mother had taken that terrible year after the divorce. Mindlessly he recorded the drugs.

Something in the wastebasket next to the sink caught his eye. Dan pulled it out of the trash. It was a home pregnancy test. She had been telling the truth.

He slammed closed his diary and put it away.

At her desk he sorted through some papers. He spun her Rolodex, looking for names, addresses. He checked her bookshelves, found a scrapbook, and pulled it down. He thumbed through it. She came from Chicago. There were pictures of her family there. And newspaper clips, an obituary among them—an obituary of Alex's father, who, according to the paper, had died of a heart attack when she was seven.

Dan gaped at the newspaper clipping, his heart thumping wildly in his chest. Who the hell, *what* the hell, was she?

Before he left, he phoned the gynecologist whose card she had given him. He said he was a friend of Alex Forrest's. Before he got any farther, the doctor said, "Ah, you must be Dan. Congratulations."

At work, he went straight to Jimmy's office. "Got to see you," he said. "Are you free now?"

"Five minutes," Jimmy said. Then he looked up and laughed. "Take your coat off. Stay awhile."

"Five minutes," Dan said. "In the library, okay?"

He couldn't hold it in anymore. It was killing him. His chest felt tight, his gut was churning, he was short of breath. In the mahogany stacks of Miller, Goodman & Hurst's law library, he told Jimmy everything.

"So I call her doctor, right? And you know what he says? 'Congratulations!' What the hell did she tell him, Jimmy? Can you imagine what she must have said to him?"

Jimmy was sweating by the time Dan stopped for breath. He took out his pocket handkerchief, mopped his cheeks, and said, "Oh, Jesus." Then he said, "Look, what do you think would happen if you just came out and told Beth?"

Dan rubbed his gut, which was knotting up again. "Are you kidding? That'd be the *end*. This woman is having my goddamn baby! Beth could never accept that. Nobody could." He ran his hands through his hair. "Anyway, Jimmy, you haven't heard it all yet. That's not the end. You know where I called her doctor from? Her place. I broke into her place this morning. I know . . . *Me*, a lawyer, breaking and entering."

"Jesus Christ," Jimmy said. "Are you crazy? Why?"

"How should I know? I was looking for something, *anything* to give me a handle on what the hell I'm dealing with here. I thought maybe I could find out if she was sleeping with anyone else. . . ."

He heard a noise and stopped. A clerk was wheeling a book cart through the stacks. Dan grabbed onto a shelf and stood there, with his head down, trying to slow his breathing, until the guy moved out of hearing range.

"I came up with nothing," he whispered urgently. "Jimmy, I've never touched family law. What kind of case does she have?"

Jimmy mopped his brow. "It ain't good," he answered. "In New York State, the law will take a woman's word for paternity until the child is born and paternity can be tested."

Dan whistled softly.

"Yeah," Jimmy commiserated. "Until the baby comes to term, the putative father—you, pal, you the father—is responsible for all medical and maintenance costs. In other words, the law supposes you *guilty* until proven innocent."

"Thanks, buddy. You sound like a lawyer."

"Sorry," Jimmy said. And he was. So sorry he could barely look Dan in the eye. He just stood there shaking his head. Then his natural optimism surfaced again. "Hey, come on. Look, once she realizes you don't want anything to do with her, she'll decide not to go through with it. She's probably hoping you'll leave your wife."

"That's crazy," Dan said.

Jimmy pinned him with a look. "She sounds a little crazy."

Dan took a breath and nodded. "Right." Then he remembered the list he'd made. "Hildy works with shrinks, right? Jimmy, I need a favor."

Jimmy Lawrence looked at his face, which was haggard with pain and anxiety. "Anything, baby," he said.

"I wrote down the names of the pills she takes. I know a couple of them. They're antidepressants. I don't know about the rest, though. Maybe she's sick. Maybe she's dying for all I know. I just want to find out . . . anything I can."

"Sure," Jimmy said. "Give me the list. I'll tell Hildy it's one of my cases. I get nut jobs like you wouldn't believe. No problem. One of the psychiatrists at the clinic can help her. They've probably got a *PDR* at work. I'll ask her what she thinks we're dealing with here."

"She keeps calling the apartment. Every time Beth answers, she hangs up. I'm scared, Jimmy. I really am. I don't want to lose my family."

"Have the number changed. Shit, call the phone company today and get an unlisted number."

"I will. Thanks." Dan turned away, afraid of showing the desperation welling inside him at the thought of Beth, of Ellen. "I don't want to lose my family," he said.

· "Listen, Dan, can I ask you something? I'd really like to understand. I know you. You don't fuck around. How come? Why'd you do it?"

"That's funny. *She* keeps asking me that. If I'm so happy, how come I went home with her?" Dan shrugged, walked over to the window, and looked out. "All I can think of is a combination lock," he said. "You know, all the tumblers have to fall into place."

"I don't get it," Jimmy said.

"If I hadn't been married ten years—*click*. If I hadn't gone to that weekend meeting—*click*. If Beth and Ellen hadn't been in the country, hadn't gone away—*click*." Dan turned back to Jimmy, who was listening intently.

"If she hadn't been at the meeting—*click*. If it hadn't been raining so hard," he continued, "if she hadn't been so attractive, so pretty—*click, click, click*! you know . . . Aw, shit, Jimmy, I don't know. I think everyone's got some combination that'll open them up . . . that can unlock them."

—— 9 ——

Dan got his home phone changed to an unlisted number. He refused Alex's calls at the office. He tried desperately to catch up on the work piling up on his desk and to not jump with apprehension every time the office phone rang. Each night he took home a briefcase crammed with work and returned, early the next morning, with less than half of it handled. He was flooded with dread and bailing with a thimble. It was all he could do for the moment. That and get his family out of the city, fast.

A couple of days before the closing on the house, Dan was so preoccupied that he stepped off the curb at West End Avenue and was brought back to reality, in the middle of the street, by the furious honking of an oncoming car.

He was still shaking as he turned the key in his apartment lock. The door was open. He walked in and heard women's voices coming from the living room. He put his briefcase down quietly in the entry hall and looked through the mail. And suddenly his spine bristled with terror.

Dan set down the mail and moved toward the voices with wild trepidation. His heart was beating so loudly, he could hardly hear what the women were saying. He caught a phrase or two. They were talking about babies.

Beth stood up to greet him. "Hi, darling," she said. "This is Alex—I'm sorry . . ." She turned to the well-dressed woman sitting on the sofa holding a half-full coffee cup. "I've forgotten your last name," Beth said.

Alex looked up at him and smiled. "Alex Forrest," she said, holding his gaze. "Hi."

"Alex Forrest," Beth said, "My husband, Dan."

Dan moved forward, without will, almost in slow motion. As if he were caught up in a bad dream, he watched Alex set her cup down on the coffee table and give him that smile, that big dazzling smile. "Glad to meet you," she said.

He glanced at Beth. She gave him a prompting nod. "Nice to meet you," he recited.

Alex got to her feet and extended her hand to him. Dan had no alternative but to shake it. She held on to him a fraction longer than necessary, studying him with exaggerated curiosity.

The blood was pounding in his ears. The sight of her smile, the way she cocked her head and appeared to be appraising him now, infuriated him, terrified him. He must have tightened his grip on her hand, because he saw her wince. She withdrew her hand quickly and massaged it, as if she were still deep in thought.

"Haven't we met before?" she asked. "Your face is awfully familiar."

"I don't think so," he heard himself say.

"No, no, we have," she persisted, her eyes twinkling, holding his. "Weren't you at a party at that Japanese place a few weeks ago? A book launch."

"Oh, darling," Beth said, "the exercise book."

"Oh, yeah . . . Yes," he muttered.

"You're a lawyer, right? You work for that firm . . . what's the name now . . . ?"

"Miller, Goodman and Hurst," Beth said.

How far was she going to go? Dan wondered. How much of his life would she "remember" standing here, in his living room, in front of his wife?

"Anyway," she concluded suddenly, "we definitely met."

"You have an excellent memory," he said, with hard-won civility.

Alex laughed at him. "I never forget a face."

Beth looked from Alex to Dan. He smiled at her, feeling ugly and weak and deeply ashamed. She had sensed something, he was sure of it. But it was not evident in her words, which were friendly, conversational, appropriate:

"It's a small world."

"It certainly is," Alex echoed, looking significantly at Dan.

There was a pause, a slight awkwardness. Beth looked to Dan to fill it. He had nothing to say. Finally Alex broke the silence. "So . . . I gather you're moving to the country?" she said, turning to him.

"Yes," Beth said.

"Have you found somewhere?" She was still staring at him, asking him directly now, as if they were alone, as if Beth were not there.

Dan didn't answer.

Beth said, "We're buying a house in Mount Kisco, up near Bedford. Have you ever been out there?"

"Yes, it's beautiful," Alex responded. "So you'd be ready to move out of here almost immediately?" she asked Beth.

Beth turned to him for guidance, but he

was useless, impassive. He'd lost the ability to even fake a smile. His face, he knew, must be a frozen mask.

"We were planning to get some remodeling done first," Beth said, beginning to clear the coffee service, picking up after Alex, putting her lipstick-rimmed cup and wet teaspoon back on the tray. "I guess you're looking for a place to move into right away?"

Dan's heart sank as he watched his wife cleaning up after Alex Forrest. She had fixed coffee for Alex, had waited on her, served her. Beth had been hospitable, open, and loving. And he had foisted this humiliation on her with his stupidity and cowardice.

"Well, I would really," Alex continued the charade. "I want to settle in."

Now, Dan thought. Tell the truth now. He glanced at Beth, who was smiling, confident, utterly innocent. He saw in his mind how that smile would fade, turn into a gasp . . . in front of Alex, the last person in the world who ought to witness Beth's pain.

Beth turned to him. "Alex is expecting a baby," she said.

It was over. The moment had passed. His resolution and his anger peaked and dissolved, leaving him drained, tired, and defeated.

"Oh . . ." he said stiffly. "Would you excuse me? I have some calls to make." He turned his back on her.

"Goodness, I've got to run," Alex said after a beat, moving to the armchair over which her coat lay, moving into Dan's peripheral vision, picking up her coat and gloves and slipping them on.

Dan didn't look at her. He leaned forward, holding on to the back of his desk chair, and stared at the letter bins of the big rolltop desk. He refused to allow Alex to catch his eye again, to give him one more saccharine smile, one more significant glance. He looked down, watching his hands gripping the back of the chair, watching his knuckles turn white.

"Thank you for the tea," Alex was saying. "And for showing me the apartment."

"Oh, you're welcome," Beth said warmly.

"I like it." She was using her sensible voice now, her grown-up, reasonable voice "I like it a lot."

"We've been very happy here," Beth said.

Dan's stomach knotted.

"I'd definitely like to think about it, if I could . . ."

He knew what was coming next. He tightened his grip on the chair.

"Let me give you our number," Beth said, coming over to the desk. She stroked Dan's back briefly, affectionately, then wrote out their new, unlisted phone number on a piece of notepaper and carried it over to Alex. "Here you are," Beth said. "So you can call us, if you want to."

"Thank you," Alex said.

They left the room. Dan ran his trembling hands through his hair. He heard them move to the door. He looked up. Through the arched doorway leading to the hall, he caught a glimpse of Alex. She was looking right at him. "I'll be in touch," she said.

He walked to the window and stared blindly out at the city. Beth turned and picked up the coffee tray.

"She seems really interested. It's funny, she didn't mention a husband. I got the feeling she's on her own."

He looked over his shoulder at her and saw, in her quick puzzlement, that his emotions were showing. Beth set down the tray and moved toward him.

"What's up?" she asked gently. "You seem depressed."

He tried to smile. "I'm fine. Just tired. Everything's fine."

Dan called Alex at Robbins and Hart the next day. A guy answered her line. "Miss Forrest's office."

"Yes," he said, tapping a pencil on his desk, keeping rhythm with the pulsing anger he felt. "Could I speak with Miss Forrest? Dan Gallagher."

He was put on hold. The guy came back on the line. "She's in a meeting, Mr. Gallagher. Can I have her return your call?"

He thought for a moment. No. He'd instructed Martha not to take Alex's calls. He didn't want to complicate it any further. "No," he said, feeling thwarted. "I'll call her back."

He knew she'd been there, in her office. He knew she was giving him a taste of his own medicine. It was a game to her, some sick damn game. He slammed down the receiver and threw the pencil across the room.

He tried her twice more that morning and got the same simpering assistant, and the same phony message.

"How're you holding up?" Jimmy looked in on him after lunch.

"I'm . . . It's incredible," he said. "I can't . . . You won't believe what she did yesterday."

"I believe, I believe. Hildy went over that medication list you gave me. . . . This is not a paragon of stability we are dealing with. What did she do?"

Dan told him.

"I don't believe it," Jimmy said, stunned.

"What did Hildy say about the pills?"

"Not good. Ups, downs, tranquilizers, speed, sleeping pills, antidepressants, mood elevators . . . a regular psychiatric pharmacopoeia."

"Oh, Jesus, Jimmy." Dan's chest began heaving, but he still felt as though he couldn't get a breath. "I walked right into it, didn't I? Eyes wide open—"

"Eyes wide open . . . with cataracts," Jimmy commiserated. "Hey, look, a sick mind is the ultimate concealed weapon, isn't it?"

Dan called Robbins and Hart again at three. This time Alex's assistant said that she'd gone home for the day. Dan asked when she'd left. The assistant said just before lunch, yes, he was sure Miss Forrest was at home. He'd just gotten off the phone with her.

Dan tried her home number three times that afternoon. Her answering machine was on. He tried her at home again after six. Same message. He left his office around seven-thirty and, impulsively, phoned Beth from a pay phone on the street.

"Hi, sweetheart," he said. "I've got to have a drink with a client. I'm going to be a little late. Not very late, though. Beth," he said, "listen . . . No, nothing . . . I love you, that's all. Give Ellen a kiss."

He took the subway uptown and tried Alex twice more—once from a phone on the Fourteenth Street Station and a few minutes later from a booth two blocks from her loft.

Same message: *Hi, I'm not in right now, but if you care to leave a message I'll call you right back.* The sound of her voice, lilting and smug, enraged him.

She was there. He was certain of it. He stopped across the street from the loft and looked up at her windows. The lights were on. He waited. Then, finally, he made up his mind, crossed the street, and went up to the entrance.

He pressed her bell. And waited. He pressed it again. Startling him, her voice came over the intercom. "Hello?"

"It's me," Dan said.

"Who?" Alex asked after a pause.

He exploded. "You know who it is! Let me in, Alex. I want to talk to you."

"Oh," she said. "Now you want to talk!"

"Yeah, I want to. Right now!"

She buzzed him in. He bolted up the stairs and banged on her door.

Alex was expecting him. The realization, the sight of her, jarred Dan. She opened the door dressed in a thin silk robe. She posed in the doorway, stood smiling at him with one hand on her hip, pulling back her sheer robe to reveal the lacy white teddy underneath. A pink bow, holding a tiny silk rosebud, pinched the center of the teddy's low-cut bosom and lay against her pale, barely concealed breasts. Tendrils of curls cascaded wildly from the knot of blond hair piled on her head.

She had known he would come. She moved aside with an ironic little smile to let him enter.

Tight-lipped, Dan followed her into her living room. She signaled for him to sit. He remained standing as she walked over to the kitchen area.

"What can I get you?" she asked. "I've got scotch, I've got vodka—there's a nice Chablis in the refrigerator. . . ."

"Can we please cut the bullshit!" he said, his anger bubbling over. "Can we just cut the bullshit now? I don't know what you're up to, but I'm telling you, it's going to stop. Right here. Right now!"

"No," Alex said calmly, turning to face him. She leaned back against the kitchen counter. "It's not going to stop. It's going to go *on* and *on* until you face your responsibilities."

"What responsibilities?" Gallagher demanded.

"I'm pregnant. I'm having our child."

"Alex, that's your choice. Not mine."

"I just want to be a small part of your life," she said.

"And you think this is the right way to go about it . . . ? Showing up at my apartment?"

She sighed and started back toward him. "What am I supposed to do? You won't talk to me. You change your number. I won't be ignored, Dan."

He shook his head. "You just don't get it, do you?" he asked coldly.

She was face-to-face with him now. She looked into his eyes. She licked her lips and lifted her face up to his. "Don't you remember our weekend?" she said softly. "Wasn't that wonderful? Why can't we be like that again?"

He studied her face, searching for some sign that she'd heard him, understood what he had said. Her denial was frightening and infuriating.

She pressed herself against him, coiling her arm around his neck. "I know you feel it, too. You want me. I know you do. . . ."

She moved her parted lips up to his, waiting for him to kiss. He pushed her away. "Don't flatter yourself," he said.

"Poor darling! You can't help having dirty thoughts, can you?"

She had mistaken his inaction for complicity, for lust. She thought he wanted her. Dan watched her now with a sickening coldness, a mixture of disgust and thinly controlled rage.

"Poor little Beth," Alex continued relentlessly. "I thought she was awfully sweet . . . but she was also kind of boring. Is she boring in bed, too? That's the problem isn't it?"

Dan grabbed her wrist and yanked her arm away from him. He held her like that, with her arm twisted up. For a second she saw the rage in his eyes, and he saw fear in hers.

"I'm warning you. You leave her out of it, Alex."

She grinned maliciously. "Go ahead, hit me!" she taunted. "If you can't fuck me, why don't you hit me?"

He let go of her. "You're so sad. You know that? You're sad and lonely—"

"Don't you pity me!" she screeched suddenly. "*Ever!* You smug bastard."

"I do pity you. You're a very sick girl."

"Why?" she screamed at him. "Because I won't let you treat me like some slut you can bang a couple of times then dump in the trash can? I'm going to be the mother of your child! I want some respect!"

"You want respect?" He stopped himself. He spun on his heels and walked toward the door. It was enough. He'd had enough.

"What are you doing?" Alex wailed. She rushed after him. "I'm sorry, Dan. Please, I didn't mean it," she begged. She caught up with him in the hall and grabbed his coat sleeve. "Please. You can't go. Please, Dan. Don't leave me."

He pushed her away and continued toward the door. She rushed after him. She threw herself at him, trying to wedge herself between him and the door.

"I'll tell your wife," she screamed.

Something inside him snapped. He grabbed her by the throat and shoved her up against the wall, pressing harder and harder.

"Do that," he said hoarsely, "and I'll kill you. I swear to God." His hand clamped murderously around her throat. He released his grip and she slumped to the floor, gasping for breath.

Dan stepped over her, opened the door, and slammed it shut behind him.

He was sweating and shaking. He leaned back against the door to catch his breath. Alex pounded the door suddenly from inside the apartment. "All it takes is a phone call, Dan," she shrieked, banging on the door. "I'm warning you, I won't just disappear!"

Dan waited. He heard her scrambling to her feet. Heard her feet pounding on the varnished wooden floors, rushing away from the door. He heard the telephone fall off a table. And Alex shouting: "That's all it takes! Eight-Seven-four-nine-six—"

She was calling out his number, dialing it, punching the buttons. . . .

There was a moment's silence. Dan waited, waited for his life to be over, waited to hear Alex say, "Hello, Beth, this is Alex Forrest. I have something to tell you—"

Silently he counted the rings, imagined his home phone ringing and Beth hurrying to answer it . . . hurrying from the kitchen, where she'd be finishing up Ellen's dinner, or from the bathroom, hurrying, leaving Ellen alone in the tub. . . .

But there was only silence, punctuated by Alex's heavy breathing.

Then, suddenly, she slammed down the telephone receiver. She must have ripped the phone out of the wall. Dan heard it smash up against the door. And then he heard Alex's anguished wail of pain, which broke, finally, into uncontrollable, violent sobbing.

—— 10 ——

The sound of her sobbing haunted Dan.
Sometimes it evoked pity in him, sometimes
fear, sometimes relief, as if it had been the
sound of a fever breaking. Alex had stopped
calling. She hadn't tried him at the office for
a couple of weeks. The hang-up calls at home
seemed to have stopped. And then they were
moving.

On a blindingly bright November morning,
they left the city and drove up to Bedford.
The trees were nearly bare now. But the sun
was very strong and the ground was ablaze
with the flaming harvest of fall. Despite the
season, it felt as though nature was on their
side and that it was a growing, not a dying
time. A new beginning.

Beth's mother was at the house with the movers when Gallagher and company arrived. Quincy shot from the car and took off after a mystery rodent, a squirrel or chipmunk or field mouse. He tore around to the back of the house and tumbled down the hill in an ecstasy of freedom. Ellen, ducking under a couch the movers were carrying up the front walk, followed him.

Gallagher tossed his jacket down in the kitchen and wandered once through the house before rolling up his sleeves to help the movers. He stopped in the living room, where Beth and Joan were ankle deep in crumpled newspapers and excelsior, unpacking hip high wooden crates. He put his arms around Beth's waist and she leaned back against him, hugging his arms and sighing.

"What a mess," he said sympathetically.

"Uh-oh." Beth nodded toward the front door, where two of the moving men were struggling with a mattress. "You'd better help out."

"I still think you were crazy to move in before the remodeling was done," Joan Rogerson said. "You could've stayed in the apartment."

Beth shrugged and pulled an old photo album out of a crate. "Dan couldn't wait to get out of New York, Mom," she said, passing the album to Joan, "is this you? That's sweet!"

Dan wove his way through the cartons and crates to the entry hall.

He pulled a table out of the movers' way and ducked down under the mattress. He was outside, trying to help push the mattress through the door, when the telephone rang. He stopped, frozen with a sudden premonition.

Beth glanced over to the far end of the room, where the phone rested on the hall stairs. She started toward it.

Scrambling back under the mattress, Dan banged his head on the table leg. "I'll get it!" he called, rubbing his head and rushing to the phone. "I've got it, honey."

Surprised by his eagerness, Beth stopped in her tracks.

Dan reached the phone on the fourth ring. He grabbed the receiver. "Hello!" he demanded. Then he smiled. "It's okay," he told Beth. "It's Martha." He grinned happily. "Martha! Martha, it's you! Yes. What is it? It's Martha," he said again. "She's just calling to give me my calls."

The day before Ellen's sixth birthday, Dan relented on the rabbit. At lunch time he grabbed a cab uptown to a pet shop on Lexington Avenue and picked out the quintessential floppy-eared, pink-eyed, fluffy-tailed beast. He carried it back to the office in a spiffy, paper-lined cage that had set him back twice the price of the rabbit.

Then he called Beth. The phone rang and rang. He waited, and found his stomach tightening with apprehension. He looked at his watch. It was too early for her to be picking Ellen up at school. . . . She had said she'd be working on the upstairs hallway today. She was supposed to be there, painting. The phone was in their bedroom, just a couple of steps away. Seven rings. Why wasn't the answering machine picking up?

"Hello?" Beth said breathlessly.

"Hi, babe." He kept it light and breezy. "Where were you?"

"Outside. How's it going?"

"Fine, everything's great. Did the plumber ever come?"

"Did he ever."

"I know. Don't tell me. I don't want to hear."

"I just walked him to the truck. It looks like a Chevy pickup, but I know it's a Rolls Royce in disguise."

"Hey," Dan said, brightening suddenly. "Guess what I'm looking at?"

She guessed. "You got it?" she said excitedly. "The rabbit!"

"I picked it up—excuse me," he said, "I picked *her* up at the store a little while ago."

"What's she like?"

"She's a rabbit. White. Long floppy ears, little eyes. No, she's beautiful. Are you sure Ellen doesn't know anything about it?"

"No. She's sure she isn't going to get one. God," Beth said. "It's nearly three. I'd better go pick her up. I'm a mess. My face, my hair. I'm all splattered with paint."

"Get any on the hallway? What an industrious woman. How's it look?"

"Ceiling's almost done. Dan, it looks great. I love our house."

"I love you. And Miss Fluffy loves you, too," he said, reaching into the cage to stroke the rabbit. "Tell the birthday girl we'll be home early tonight."

He packed his briefcase at five.

"I like your friend," Eunice said as he carried the cage past the reception area on his way out.

He showed her the rabbit. "Have you met our new partner? Be careful, Eunice," Dan kidded. "This is what happens to you if you stay here too long—they carry you out in a cage. Right, Fluffs?"

"Aren't we sweet?" Eunice cooed at the rabbit. "Oh, I forgot." She turned to Dan. "This arrived for you." She handed him a small padded envelope. He slipped it into his pocket, thanked her, and left.

The first odd thing he noticed was that the

garage attendant's booth was empty. A small portable TV played to a vacant chair. "Hey, Joachin!" Gallagher called. When there was no answer, he leaned into the booth and took his keys from the rack.

"Where's Joachin? Hey, Fluffy? Have you seen Joachin?"

Talking to the rabbit, he walked over to the elevator. "They're going to take us both away, Miss Fluffs, they catch me talking to you. Yes, they are." He got into the elevator and pressed the third-floor button.

The car rose slowly past half-empty cement-slab floors painted with parking spaces. Dan called out to Joachin again on the second floor. There was no answer. He got out at the third, feeling a little spooked by the silence.

A car alarm went off, startling him. Dan jumped. "Jesus. Sorry, kiddo," he told the jarred rabbit. "What is that smell? Miss Fluffy, say it isn't you."

Dan was smiling as he turned the corner. He slowed down suddenly. The smile froze grotesquely on his face. Ahead of him, a poisonous, hissing vapor rose in a yellowy cloud from his car.

He approached slowly, hardly able to believe his eyes. The paint was blistering and peeling off the BMW's metal. The metal itself was dissolving, dribbling over the windows in a hideous molten mass.

The stench was unbearable—hydrochloric acid. It had been poured over the entire car, giving off a sinister, hissing steam as it ate away at the body of the BMW.

A shadow moved on the ramp above him. Dan looked up and caught a swirl of dark fabric, a coat or dress, then heard staccato footsteps echoing through the garage.

He knew who it was. He knew who had committed the demented act. Before he saw the shadow or heard the footsteps, he knew it was Alex Forrest and, in the dark garage, Dan roared with rage.

Terror returned as his brain tried to make sense of the senseless violation. Did it have anything to do with Ellen's birthday? Had Alex chosen the day deliberately? Was it a random choice or was she trying to stop him from getting home tonight?

He rushed to the phone. Everything was fine, Beth assured him. She was upset about the car.

"What sort of fire, Dan?" she asked. "I don't understand."

"Electrical. It had something to do with the electrical system," he said. "The whole thing went up in smoke. I'm going to take care of things here. Then I'll rent a car and get home as soon as possible, okay?"

At the car-rental place, as Dan went through

his coat pockets looking for change, he found the package that had been left for him at the reception desk. He turned it over in his palm, then tossed it into the front seat of the rental car and climbed in for the long ride home.

He didn't glance at it again until he hit the stop-and-go traffic of the toll plaza. Then he picked it up and, with sudden intuition, tore it open. It was a cassette with the words *Play Me* scrawled on it. Dan stared at it for a moment. Someone behind him honked. He started up his car again and put the cassette into the deck.

Hello Dan. Surprised? I guess you thought you'd get away with it. This is what you've reduced me to.

The sound of Alex's voice infuriated him, sickened him. He snapped it off. His jaw was clenched. His fingers were tight around the wheel of the car. His anger was dangerous. It was pounding in his head and gut. He wanted to slow down, to pull over to the side of the road for a minute. He glanced into the rearview mirror and, suddenly, he thought he saw her. The wild curls, the determined set of her head . . . She was in a white Honda, two cars back in the next lane.

The sight unnerved him. The car beside him honked and he realized he was easing too far to the left. He straightened out, then took the turn. When he looked into the mirror again, the Honda had dropped back. A van pulled behind him, obscuring his view. By the time the van passed him, the Honda was gone. Gallagher reached forward and hit the tape player again.

Well, you were wrong.

Was she on her way up to his house? Did she know where they lived now? He checked his rearview mirror several more times, but Alex—if it had been Alex—was nowhere in sight.

Part of you is growing inside me. That's a fact, Dan—and you'd better start learning how to deal with it.

As the threatening voice droned, Dan found himself bargaining with God. Let it just be the car, he prayed. Let it just be . . . whatever it was—a desperate impulsive act, an insane attempt at revenge. I can live with that, he thought. I can live without a car, a goddamn car, a piece of metal. Only, dear God, let me get home fast and find my family safe.

In the backseat, the rabbit ruffled the newspapers in her cage, and Gallagher jumped. He shook his head and tried to listen to the tape again because maybe it would tell him what she wanted, what she was up to.

Her voice had changed. Her mood had shifted. She sounded lonely now and full of longing.

Oh, Dan, I feel you. I taste you. I think you, and touch you. . . . Can you understand? Can you?

After a while, she sighed. When she spoke again, the sadness had given way to anger.

I'm asking you to acknowledge your responsibilities! You are going to be a father. A father has certain responsibilities to his child. I'm just asking that you behave responsibly. Is that unreasonable? I don't think so!

He listened. She seemed increasingly agitated. Her words began to slur. She cursed him. She professed her love. She tried to sound reasonable, sensible, and almost succeeded for a few seconds at a time.

He ejected the tape, yanked out the cassette, and shoved it in his jacket pocket. He pulled into the gravel driveway of his home and sat in the car for a few seconds, trying to compose himself. Finally he reached back for the rabbit cage.

A car cruised slowly past the driveway entrance. He caught a glimpse of it, then it disappeared behind the trees lining the road. He thought it was a white car. Could it have been the Honda? He looked quickly up at his house. It was peaceful. The lights were on downstairs. He saw Beth move past the big picture window in the living room. She was carrying a glass of milk. She bent down and he lost sight of her behind the silhouetted shrubs outside the window.

Once outside, he saw that she and Ellen were kneeling on the floor in front of a log fire, working on a giant jigsaw puzzle. Ellen was in her pajamas, ready for bed.

"Hey, what's a guy got to do to get a hug around here?" he asked.

"Daddy!" Ellen shouted, scrambling instantly to her feet. Then she saw the rabbit. Her eyes widened in disbelief. She covered her mouth with her plump little hand and gasped. "A rabbit," she said.

"Met it on the way home," Dan said, setting down the cage. "It was hitching along the Taconic. Asked me did I know a six-year-old named Ellen. So I gave it a lift."

"Oh, you!" Ellen said, running into his outstretched arms. She gave him a generous, happy hug, then scrambled down to peer into the rabbit's cage. "Oh, he's so cute," she breathed, suddenly awestruck. "Mom," she whispered. "Mom, come here and look at him."

Beth was beaming at Dan. He smiled back at her. He was tired but trying not to let the strain show. It was as if seeing them, knowing finally that they were all right, had given his mind and body permission to feel again. What he felt was enormous exhaustion.

"I'm going to call him Whitey."

Dan took off his coat and turned to toss it into the armchair near the picture window. "I think it's a she, baby," he said to Ellen. And then he stopped cold. The hair on the back of his neck bristled.

Through the dark window, he saw a face. Out in the moonlight, someone was watching.

Fear set his heart pounding. His mind raced wildly. Alex Forrest *had* followed him home. She was standing outside now, there, just beyond the shrubbery, between the house and the big elm tree on the front lawn. She was moving toward him, coming close to the window.

Without warning, Beth went to the window and pulled the curtains shut. Gallagher turned, waiting to hear her say, *Call the police, Dan. Hurry!* But she was smiling at him. Beth was calm and smiling. Then her smile wavered and she said, "Dan, are you all right?"

He nodded, tried to smile.

"You look so tired," Beth said. "Are you hungry?"

It wasn't until they were sitting around the dinner table together that he figured out what had happened. It was Beth he'd seen. She'd moved toward the window to shut the curtains and, in his stressed-out state, he'd seen her reflection in the dark window and mistaken it for someone outside. A woman, of course. Alex.

He needed sleep. He needed a hot shower and a good night's sleep. But first he wanted to listen to the rest of the tape. He had to find out what Alex wanted now—and why she'd destroyed the car. And what she might do next.

After dinner, he went up to his "study," the beautifully transformed attic, which Beth had lovingly remodeled for him. He sat at his desk, and put on his earphones, and took Alex's cassette out of his jacket pocket. And, alone, in the quiet house, he listened.

You thought you could just walk into my life and turn it upside down without a thought for anyone but yourself. You know what you are. . . ?

Alex's voice was thick, her words slurred.

You're a cocksucking son-of-a-bitch, Dan. I'll bet you don't even really like girls. They probably scare you. I know I do. Boo, Dan. Careful, you'll have a heart attack, you sick motherfucker. . . .

Gallagher stared straight ahead, listening, lost.

No one leaves me, you shit! No one walks out on me. They get carried out. Ask my fucking father, that dumb bastard. I wished he would die. And you know what, Dan? He did. Right before my eyes. Because I wanted him to!

A pair of hands slipped over his shoulders. He tore off the earphones and pressed the off button on the tape deck.

"Jesus, you scared the shit out of me." He hadn't heard Beth come up the stairs.

She was startled, too. "Sorry," she said, taking a step back. "I was just wondering what you were doing."

"Oh," he said, massaging his chest. "I was just . . . listening to a deposition. I guess I'm still upset about the car, needed to unwind. . . ."

Beth smiled. "Come on, I'll give you a back rub," she said. She put her arm around him and led him to the stairs. "A back rub and a brandy and you won't know what hit you," she promised.

—— 11 ——

Dan got up early the next morning and went downstairs with Quincy whimpering at his heels. He let the golden retriever out and stood at the door watching him for a moment or two.

He hadn't slept well. The tape had gotten to him. There was no doubt in his mind now that Alex Forrest was very sick and that she was responsible for the insane act of destruction in the garage yesterday. What further violence she might be capable of Dan wasn't sure, but something needed to be done.

He wasn't going to spend the rest of his life or even the rest of the week looking over his shoulder, waiting for her next move. He had caught about three hours of fitful sleep and, at first light of dawn, he'd almost made up his mind.

While Quincy sniffed and rolled and barked his good mornings to the world, Dan went back upstairs and showered and shaved quietly and dressed for work. Beth stirred. He told her it was too early for her to be up. He said he wanted to get into the office, that there was a lot to do, and that he had to stop at the garage on his way in, to check on the car.

Of course, there was no garage to stop at; there was no car. It was at the pound, a mutilated wreck. Dan went to the front door and called to Quincy, but the dog wanted to play. He ran toward the house and stopped. He whimpered and barked, inviting Dan to join him, then ran into the bushes in front of the picture window.

"Come on, boy," Dan called, but he let Quincy draw him out into the new morning. He picked up the ratty tennis ball lying next to the front walk and tossed it. Quincy took off after it like a shot.

Dan was grateful for the moment of normalcy, for the crisp air and country noises, for the prickly fall grass across which Quincy bolted. He spotted some crumpled paper on the lawn and, in his new lord-of-the-manor mode, marched toward the affronting sight.

Tissues. He found a handful of tissues near the shrubs in front of the picture window and, when he stooped to pick them up, discovered that someone had thrown up on the lawn. His first thought was that Quincy had eaten grass or worse and gotten sick.

Then he thought about the tissues and laughed at himself. Quincy was a bright dog, but not bright enough to try to clean up the mess he'd made. . . .

Dan shook his head and let it go.

It wasn't until he was pulling out of his driveway twenty minutes later that he thought of the tissues on the lawn again, and a horrifying new possibility presented itself. He saw the picture window and thought vaguely about how vulnerable it was to intruders, Peeping Toms, voyeurs. He remembered Beth drawing the curtains last night. He remembered how spooked he'd been at her reflection in the window. He remembered that he had mistaken it for Alex. And then he realized that the tissues on the lawn were close to where he thought he'd seen her standing last night—

Dan pulled off the road at Bedford and drove directly to the police station.

He didn't know exactly what he'd say. He found himself inventing a stupid story about a client. "My client wants it stopped," he found himself saying to an unnervingly calm and laconic local lieutenant. "He wants an end to the harassment."

"And he's positive it was this woman who trashed his car?" The lieutenant, Detective Lieutenant Russo, according to the name-plate on his desk, was regarding Dan thought-fully. He was a pleasant-looking man in his forties, with salt-and-pepper hair and intense dark eyes.

"Yes," Dan answered, startled. "Who else?"

"Any witnesses?" Russo asked.

"No . . ."

"Well," the lieutenant said, sitting forward, folding his hands on his desk. "He's welcome to file a complaint, if it'll make him feel any better. There's not a lot we can do, without proof."

"Look, Lieutenant . . . the woman's com-pletely irrational. There's no telling what she might do."

Russo nodded. When he realized Dan had stopped speaking, he said, "We can't go around arresting people on account of what they might do. *You* know that, counselor."

"I'm not asking . . ." Gallagher tried to clear his head. He stopped and took a deep breath. "I'm not asking you to arrest her." He caught himself. "He just wants her warned."

The lieutenant was nodding again, professionally, like a kindly social worker. "We could talk to her," he said tiredly. "It's going to make things more public, which he ain't gonna like. It may even aggravate the situation with the girl."

"What do you mean?"

"Well, whatever resentment she was feeling, she's probably got it out of her system. Any action we take may simply provoke her."

"And if she hasn't 'got it out of her system'? What then?" Dan demanded, increasingly irritated with Russo's casual approach.

"Then he," the lieutenant said pointedly, "had better catch her in the act. Then we can file charges."

Dan leaned forward. "You're saying he . . . the guy's just got to sit there and take it?" he asked incredulously.

Russo regarded him silently for a moment. Finally he said, "I'm afraid so, Mr. Gallagher. It's his bed, isn't it? I'm afraid he's going to have to lie in it."

That was Tuesday morning. The words stayed with him all day and through the night when, as if he were living the metaphor, he found that he could not lie in his bed. He could toss and turn and sit up and stare mindlessly at the TV, but sleep was impossible. And though he was working desperately to catch up, particularly on *Rogers* v. *Winitsky*, which Arthur had asked him to present to the litigation committee on Friday, he could not concentrate in bed or, for that matter, at his desk in the attic or even at work anymore.

By Friday he looked like he felt—sick with worry and exhaustion, jumpy and irritable, trapped. He sat beside Arthur Ashley at the head of the polished mahogany table in the main conference room at Miller, Goodman & Hurst, drumming his fingers nervously while Arthur addressed the litigation committee.

"And so, if everybody agrees, we'll take an immediate appeal from Judge Whitman's order denying our motion to halt the takeover bid. And if that fails, we'll seek an expedited trial."

Arthur looked around the table for agreement from the firm's partners and most experienced trial lawyers, who met once a month to review pretrial strategies in each of Miller, Goodman & Hurst's major cases.

"Now, with regard to *Rogers* versus *Winitsky*," he continued, nodding at Gallagher, "Dan has what I think is a bold stroke. It's a gamble but worth taking—and that is to go for summary judgment. I've asked Dan to give us the gist of his argument and then we can discuss details. Dan?"

Arthur turned the meeting over to him.

Dan awoke from his daydream with a start. "Uh, yes," he said, opening his briefcase, realizing that he should have opened it discreetly awhile ago and gotten his notes together. "Thank you, Arthur. Just to bring you all up to speed . . . let me just recap here a minute on this Rogers case."

What the hell had he been thinking of? Was he going to try to wing it now, in front of the honchos? His career was on the line here.

"Rogers is accusing Winitsky of plagiarizing an article . . . by Winitsky . . . of course."

He fished nervously in his attaché case, talking fast to cover his search for the brief . . . which, with a sinking heart, he was beginning to realize he might have forgotten. And not just left it on his desk two flights downstairs—a circumstance that would look dumb but could at least be remedied. But that he'd left it at home. Next to the bed. Left it where he'd thrown it in frustration last night when he'd gone downstairs to pace the living room and peer continuously out the window to see if anyone was standing out there in the dark, watching him, watching his family, waiting.

"I'm sorry, Arthur, I seem to have left . . . I don't seem to have the papers for the appeal here with me, not right in front of me."

They were all watching him, waiting. Arthur made no secret of his annoyance. "Jesus, Dan," he said, "the litigation committee only meets once a month!"

Dan's palms were sweating. His hands were shaking. He glanced once around the table. Not a smile, not a sympathetic shrug, not an ounce of understanding. The inner sanctum was united in impatience and disdain.

"Arthur," he said, shutting his briefcase, "I know. I blew it. I'm sorry." He turned to the waiting partners. "I'm sorry," he said once more.

Arthur nodded curtly to him, then by way of dismissal, began rearranging his papers. "All right. Moving on to the *Forsythe* versus *Plimpton*. Does anybody feel that we ought to be challenging the precedents set by the Federal Appeals Court ruling in *Harrison* versus *McDonald* . . . ?"

Beth knew something was wrong. "Is it the house, Dan?" she asked on Saturday morning. "Did I rush you into it? I thought I'd just wait until we'd settled in for a bit before I looked into teaching, but—"

"No," he said. "It's just work. I've got a

huge caseload suddenly. And . . . I'm a little rundown, that's all. Probably flu, a cold, nothing, Beth, really."

"If you'd rather stay home," she offered.

"Hell, no." He found the strength to fake a laugh. And he went out back to call Ellen.

She was racing down the hill with carrots in her hand and Quincy hot on her heels.

"Here Whitey, here Whitey!" she shouted, as if she expected the caged rabbit to meet her halfway.

Dan followed her down the hall and stopped a few feet away to watch. Ellen fell to her knees and peered into the lopsided wooden hutch he and Jimmy had built on Wednesday night. Hildy was visiting her mother in Florida and Jimmy Lawrence had begged Dan for an invitation to dinner. Dan knew that the request—"Come on, Gallagher. Left to my own resources, I could get into twice as much trouble as you. Hey, by weight alone, *four* times as much!"—was a gesture of love and support from the big guy who knew how emotionally wiped out Gallagher was. And Beth had been thrilled when the boisterous Jimmy pulled into the driveway.

"Okay, now, Whitey, you be good till we get back," Ellen was saying. "We're going to Grandma Joan's house and you can't come yet. But if you be good, when you grow up, you can. Right, Quincy? When Quincy was a puppy, he had to stay home, too."

"Let's go, gorgeous," Dan said.

"Say good-bye to Whitey, Daddy!"

"So long, Fluffer," he said. "Come on, Quincy. Let's get this menagerie on the road."

At Joan and Howard's, Dan sat in the alcove off the large living room having a leisurely drink and chatting with his father-in-law. Howard's Madison Avenue war stories were always easy to take and Dan felt himself begin to loosen up, begin to relax.

Still, he kept an eye on Beth and Ellen. It had become second nature. He needed to know where they were and how they were. He had to restrain himself from calling home too often during the day. He had to come up with resourceful excuses to call.

But today was special. Today they were together, safe, happy. and he could hear his daughter rehearsing for her role in the first-grade play.

"I see you didn't get your car back," Howard said unexpectedly.

It brought Dan up short. He glanced at his father-in-law and saw that he was looking out the window at the rental car in the driveway.

Dan took a sip of his scotch. "No. It's a write-off. The wiring's completely burnt out."

Howard shook his head. "Shame," he said. "Amazing, those foreign cars."

"Beth, darling." Joan handed Beth a cup of tea. "Here you are, dear."

"Thanks," Beth said, setting the cup down and turning again to Ellen. "You want to try it again, baby?"

"Mommy," Ellen explained with a hint of irritation, "I know my lines. You don't have to tell me."

"Okay. Let's hear it."

"Okay!" Ellen was agreeable again. Shade to sunshine in half a second. Dan loved her easy disposition. She cleared her throat. "Okay, so. 'Dear Pussilla . . . Miles ast me—' "

" '—to ask you,' " Beth prompted.

" 'To ask you to marry him.' "

"Very good! Now do it with the hat."

Ellen put on the pilgrim hat she'd made at school. It was a bit big and rested on her ears. She held it on with one hand and bowed deeply. Her tongue peeped out the corner of her mouth as she frowned in concentration.

The sight of her, small and diligent and serious, moved Dan almost to tears. He was flooded with admiration for her, with enormous pride and love.

" 'Dear Pussilla. Miles ast me to ask you to marry him!' "

" 'Speak for yourself, John!' " Beth cued

her. "That's what she'll say. Very good, honey, you got it!"

"Ellen?" Dan called. "Ellen, come here, baby . . . Give me a big hug."

Flushed with success, Ellen ran to him and he picked her up and held her tight. And, suddenly, he was overcome with emotion. His eyes filled. He turned away, but Beth had seen him.

"Are you okay?" she whispered, coming over to him.

"Yeah. I'm fine," he replied softly. "I'm okay."

"Daddy," Ellen complained, whispering, too. "You're squeezing."

"I'm worried," Beth said as they pulled into the driveway. "I think you should see a doctor. See Jeff Weissman, just for a checkup, darling. You really do look rundown."

"Thanks a lot," Dan teased her.

"I'm serious."

"Okay," he said.

She smiled. "Okay. Hey!" she hurried out of the car and turned her attention to Ellen, who'd bolted from the backseat. "Watch out for the hat! Quincy's going after it," she called as Ellen ran around to the back of the house to check on Whitey.

Gallagher sat in the car for a minute or two. "Dan, could you lug the little toolbox in from the garage when you come, please?" Beth called back to him.

He remained behind the wheel, staring through the windshield. Then he let out a deep sigh and opened the door, wiping the dampness from his palms.

"Mommy! Mommy!" he heard Ellen shriek suddenly. Gallagher leaped from the car and raced around to the back of the house.

"What, baby? I'm here," he called. "What's the matter?"

She was running up the hill from the rabbit hutch. "Daddy! Whitey's gone!" she wailed.

A moment before he reached her, a piercing scream erupted from the house. Dan turned and raced toward the back door. "Beth! Beth, are you okay?" he yelled. He ran inside, swerved around the door post into the kitchen, and skidded to a stop.

Beth was standing in the middle of the kitchen screaming. Her face was buried in her hands. She was shaking uncontrollably and screaming.

"What is it? Beth, what happened!"

He heard a bubbling, gurgling noise. He turned slowly toward the stove.

Whitey's glassy eyes stared out at him from an enormous pot of boiling water. It took Dan a moment to notice the carrots. In the churning water, sliced carrots bobbed around the little rabbit in grotesque imitation of stew.

It was close to midnight before Ellen finally sobbed herself to sleep. After burying the rabbit at the far end of the yard, in a stand of evergreens, Dan had gone back up to the house to relieve Beth.

Somehow she had bathed Ellen and managed to get her into her pajamas and into bed. He kissed Beth on the forehead. With a weak smile, she stood up. "I'm going to shower," she said, and left him with his daughter.

Dan sat at the side of Ellen's bed, stroking her heaving back and smoothing her dark bangs back from her forehead. Her forehead and cheeks were flushed and wet. She was curled into a little ball, her fists locked tightly around a frayed piece of patchwork that had once been her baby blanket.

After a while, Beth returned. She had not bathed. She'd gone for a walk outside, she said. There was coffee on downstairs. She told him to go on, have a cup, go for a walk, she'd stay with Ellen now.

Dan was staring out the door into the backyard when Beth came downstairs. It had begun to rain. He was gazing blankly at the empty rabbit hutch.

"How is she? She okay?" he asked as Beth entered the kitchen.

"She's asleep. . . ." Beth crossed to the coffeepot and refilled the cup she'd carried downstairs with her. Dan noticed that her hands were still shaking.

She walked past him. "You call the police yet?" she asked, her back to him.

"Not yet . . . no," he said quietly, watching her.

"Why not?"

"Honey . . . Beth," he said. "We've got to talk."

She turned to face him, alerted by something in his voice. "What about?" she asked, holding his gaze for a moment. Then she looked away, walked away, touching his arm lovingly on her way into the living room.

Dan closed the back door and followed her.

"What is it?" she asked, sitting down on the sofa, warming her hands on the side of the cup.

He turned to face her. He took a deep breath. "I know who did this," he said.

"You do? Who?"

He closed his eyes. "Do you remember the girl who came to see the apartment? The one I, we, met . . . saw at the Japanese restaurant?"

"The girl with blond hair?"

He nodded. He opened his eyes as if that

would open his mouth, too, and make it possible for him to speak again. All he saw was Beth's fear, and for a moment he knew that it was as great as his. The same as his. She was waiting for him to tell her that their life together was over.

"You're scaring me," Beth said with a terrible, weak smile. "Why don't you talk? What is it?" She tried to laugh. "Did you have an affair with her?"

He nodded first. It wasn't enough. Finally, with difficulty, he said, "Yes."

Beth buried her head in her hands. Dan sat down opposite her, trying to hold back his own tears, his sick, self-pitying fear. "Honey, the last thing I ever wanted to do is hurt you," he managed to say. It sounded hollow. "More than anything, I didn't mean to hurt you—"

Beth shook her head, confused, stunned. "Are you in love with her?" she interrupted him.

"Of course not. It was one night. It meant nothing, believe me."

"Then why?" she said angrily. "I don't get it. What does this have to do with what happened—"

"She's pregnant," Dan said.

Beth recoiled in pain. "She's pregnant . . . and it's *yours*?"

He moved toward her, wanting to comfort her. "That's what she says. . . . Honey, she's crazy. . . . I don't know!"

"Don't come near me!" she shouted, standing suddenly.

"Please . . ." He reached out to her hopelessly. "I love you."

Horrified, Beth backed away from him, but he pursued her. Finally she began to flail at him. "Get the fuck out!" she screamed. "Just leave me alone."

"Beth. Please," he begged her. "Listen to me!"

She rushed at him again, punching and scratching his face. Dan tried to protect himself without fighting back, without hurting her.

"I hate you," she was screaming. "I want you out of here, understand? I want you *out of here! Just get the fuck out of here!*"

He grabbed her wrists and she started to kick him. Suddenly, with a gasp and a wrenching cry, she stopped. "Oh, no," she wailed. "Oh, no!"

Dan turned to look at what had stopped her, what had horrified her. It froze his heart.

Ellen was standing in the doorway, watching them. Tears were streaming down her face.

"Oh, God," Beth sobbed.

Dan packed a suitcase for himself while Beth put Ellen back to bed. He'd told the truth, finally, and his worst fears had been realized. It hadn't gotten better. He didn't feel better. There was no relief.

His heart felt weighted with lead. His head pounded. His limbs ached. He had told the truth and it hadn't lessened his pain at all. Like a virulent disease, it had merely spread to infect the two people he loved best in the world. Now Beth and Ellen shared his pain.

What had he accomplished?

He heard Beth going down the stairs. Dan closed his suitcase and carried it with him to Ellen's room. He didn't go inside. Her nightlight was on. He stood in the doorway watching her for a little while. She was asleep. Her breathing was regular, but her fragile eyelids, nearly transparent with pale purple veins, twitched restlessly.

Downstairs, Beth was sitting on the sofa. She'd switched most of the lights out. Her arms were folded across her chest and she was keening slightly, rocking very gently back and forth.

Dan walked past her to the telephone and dialed Alex Forrest's number.

"Hello?" she said.

His grip on the receiver tightened. "Hello? Alex?" he said. His voice was like ice. His hatred stabbed him violently, slashed at his chest, his lungs, like razor-sharp ice.

She said nothing for a moment. In the wary silence he could almost feel her fear, hear her mind mind race. Then, with tentative bravado, she said said ironically, "Dan. This is a pleasant surprise."

"Yeah," he said. "Well, you did it, Alex. Didn't you? Are you happy now?"

"Am I happy? Now let me see—I'll have to think about that one."

"Well, you think about it. It's all over, Alex. It's finished. I've told Beth. Beth knows all about it. She . . . I've told her," he said.

"Oh, sure," Alex Forrest said sarcastically. "You haven't got the balls."

"Why don't you speak to her."

"Why should I?" Alex said, her voice uncertain suddenly, uncomfortable. "Why should I want to talk to her?"

Dan held the receiver out to Beth. She got up and walked to the phone. He was amazed at her calmness. Her voice, when she spoke, was very cool, but there was a lethal undercurrent to her measured tone.

"This is Beth Gallagher," she said. "If you

ever come near my family again, I'll kill you. Is that understood?"

Then she hung up and, without a word, walked past him out of the living room and up the stairs.

— 12 —

Dan got back to the hotel at seven-thirty. He phoned down for his messages. There were none. He took off his coat and tossed his briefcase onto the big double bed and dialed his home number. It rang three times before Ellen picked up.

"Hello? . . . Daddy!"

She had sounded tired on the phone this morning. Dan had worried that she was coming down with something or that she wasn't sleeping well.

"Hi, honey." She sounded fine to him now. He sat down on the bed and pulled off his tie.

"Daddy . . . when are you coming home?"

"I don't know, sweetie. How're you doing?"

He reached into his briefcase, then realized that he'd forgotten to pack the picture of Beth and Ellen with the rest of the junk he'd brought back to the hotel from the office tonight.

"Fine."

"Yeah?" He cradled the phone in his neck, pulled his diary out of the briefcase, and made a note to himself about the photograph. The entry for Sunday caught his eye. *Joan & Howard/Dinner*, it said. Last Sunday. The last time he'd been with his family. Dan shut the leather diary and massaged his gut.

"Grandpa taught me a new card trick."

"The one with the jacks?" he said in his light and breezy, talking-to-Ellen tone. But he felt sick to his stomach and knew he was close to breaking down again.

"No, silly. The one with the kings."

"Oh, I see." Dan cleared his throat. "How's Mom?"

Beth would not speak to him.

"Fine."

"Will you tell her I said hello?"

"Yeah."

"Don't forget."

"I won't."

"I send you both lots of love. Both of you, okay? What are you eating?"

"A fruit roll-up," Ellen said. "Daddy, will you call me tomorrow?"

"I promise, sweetheart. Don't forget to tell Mom, okay?"

"I won't. Okay. 'Bye, Daddy."

Dan turned on the television and sat back on the bed. He stared blankly at the screen. A game show was on. He couldn't follow it, didn't try. He thought about ordering up a sandwich and a pot of coffee and tackling some of the work he'd brought home with him. Home.

He wasn't hungry. And he was too wiped out to look at work. He'd been getting into the office at seven-thirty each morning and leaving close to seven-thirty each night. It was eight-thirty now. He needed a shower and some sleep.

But he didn't get up. He knew that if he just lay there staring at the TV screen, he'd fall asleep with his clothes on again. He thought about taking his shoes off, but didn't move.

The urge to call Beth came predictably. It amazed Dan how painful a desire could be minute by minute, hour after hour. He'd have thought its potency would diminish with time and repetition. But it hadn't. He longed to hear her voice. To see her again. To work things out now.

It was going to take time, he told himself.

He told himself that every night. And every morning. Mornings were worse. Mornings he'd wake before dawn with his heart pounding and terrifying nightmares chasing him into the day. Mornings he had to get away from the phone fast so that he wouldn't call Beth.

Or Ellen. The thought of his daughter, the memory of her face as she watched Beth and him fighting, her scream when she ran into the kitchen that Sunday before he could sweep her away from the sight of the rabbit . . . It had done something to him. It had made him a little crazy, he thought. Because he felt the urge, the need, to hear her voice, to know that she was all right, constantly.

Beth was strong in some deep miraculous way. But Ellen was a baby, and vulnerable. And Dan was afraid for her.

At Beth's insistence he spoke to his daughter only twice a day now—before she left for school and before she went to bed. It took great restraint on his part. He worried about her all the time. He treasured the sound of her voice beyond reason.

It wasn't just that he loved and missed her, Dan thought; it was that without Beth to speak to, Ellen had become his sole link to life, the only life he wanted now, a normal, predictable, everyday life with his small, safe family.

Safe. That was the word that took him beyond reason. He was obsessed with his family's safety and only his daily conversations with Ellen alleviated his fears a little and sometimes kept at bay the nightmarish apprehension that haunted him.

For four days, Dan lived with his fears. On the fifth they came true.

Returning to the office from a late-afternoon meeting, he stepped off the elevator into the reception area with Harold Kennedy, one of Miller, Goodman's new young turks.

Eunice waved at them. Dan wasn't sure who she was signaling. She nodded emphatically when he pointed to himself.

"You were good in there," Kennedy was saying. "You looked so laid back . . . like you were a million miles away, but the minute Landesman said 'plagiarism,' man, you showed up like Superman out of the phone booth."

"Superman?" Dan laughed and clapped the younger man on the shoulder. "Thanks, I needed that."

"Mr. Gallagher," Eunice called. "Martha's been trying to reach you. Your wife called—"

Dan hurried down the corridor. Martha was not at her desk. He looked quickly through the yellow message slips. There were two from Joan Rogerson.

He dialed his mother-in-law's number. It rang and rang. Dan looked at his watch. It was close to six. Nothing to get nuts about, he told himself. It was Friday night. They were social, Joan and Howard. They could be anywhere.

He hung up and dialed his home. There was no answer there, either. The answering machine was on. He left a message for Beth saying he'd heard she had called and that he was back at the office now and would either be there or at the hotel or en route. "I love you," he added impulsively. "I hope you're okay."

He went round to Jimmy's office. Jimmy was packing up his briefcase. "Dan! What happened?" he asked, dropping everything and coming to Gallagher's side. "Jesus, where have you been? What's going on?"

"What do you mean?"

"With Ellen," Jimmy said. "Have they found her?"

"What!" Dan's ears rang suddenly. He heard his own voice through waves of dizziness and echoes.

"Sit down," Jimmy said. "Jesus Christ, you're white as a sheet."

Dan grabbed Jimmy's jacket. "What happened," he said, "what happened to Ellen?"

"I don't know. I thought you knew. Martha

said Beth called her. . . . She went to pick Ellen up at school and Ellen wasn't there. Someone, another kid, I think, said that Ellen had already been picked up. Beth thought maybe it was you. That you'd driven up there today instead of tomorrow. And picked her up early or something."

"No," Dan said.

"God, Dan, I'm sorry. I thought Martha told you."

"No," Dan repeated.

"Sit down," Jimmy said. "Just fucking sit down before you fall down, would you?" He poured Dan a glass of water from the carafe on his desk. "Let me see if I can find Martha." Jimmy started out of the office. "Here she is," he said, stopping at the door.

Dan did not like the look on Martha's face. She wasn't even pretending to be calm. "Dan," she said, "there's been an accident—"

"Ellen—"

"No," Martha said. "It's Beth. She's been in a car crash. She's pretty beaten up. Your mother-in-law just called from the hospital up in Bedford."

"Beth?" Dan was confused. He looked at Jimmy. For a moment he thought that Jimmy had misunderstood Martha's earlier story; that it was Beth who was missing, who hadn't picked Ellen up from school.

"Jesus Christ, this is terrible," Jimmy was saying. The news of the accident had stunned him.

"Then Ellen's okay?" Dan asked. But one look at Martha told him he was whistling in the dark. It was not Beth *or* Ellen. It was Beth and Ellen.

Dan left the city at the height of the rush hour. The hour-and-a-half trip home would take two now, even if he was lucky and there were no repairs or accidents on the road to slow things down. As it was, traffic was bumper to bumper and crawling.

He had reached Beth's mother at the hospital. Joan Rogerson was crying when she came to the phone. "Oh, Dan. Thank God. Hurry, please. She needs you. We need you, darling."

It was true. Beth had been in an accident. She'd gone to Ellen's school at three. Ellen was not there. One of the teachers was sure she'd been picked up earlier by a woman. A classmate of Ellen's had seen her get into a white car. She hadn't seen who was driving it.

As best Joan could piece it together, Beth had been frantic, driving around, searching for Ellen. She'd called Joan from home about four, to check and make certain Joan had not impulsively picked her granddaughter up at school.

Joan could hear Beth's panic and breathlessness. Ellen had not been home, Beth said. She'd searched every room of the house and run from one end of the yard to the other calling for her. She'd stopped and checked with neighbors. No one had seen Ellen.

It was Joan who had suggested calling Dan on the off chance that he'd picked his daughter up from school. Beth said she'd already call Dan's office and that he was out at a meeting.

Joan had asked Beth to wait at home until Howard could get there, just in case Ellen wandered in. But Beth was too frantic by then. She'd said she had to find Ellen at once.

"She said," Joan told Dan with a gulp of shame that should have been his, "that a friend of yours, a very sick woman, might have done something to harm Ellen. And then," Joan said, sobbing, "she told us what happened to Ellen's rabbit."

After talking to her mother, Beth had apparently gotten back in the car and gone searching for Ellen.

Joan had called the police while Howard had rushed over to the Gallaghers' house. By the time his father-in-law arrived, Beth was gone.

Within an hour Joan received a phone call from a police officer saying that her daughter had been in a traffic accident, that Beth's silver Volvo had been broadsided by a station wagon and that Beth was in intensive care at St. Michaels.

Howard was still at the Gallaghers' house, Joan said. He didn't want to leave, not even to see Beth at the hospital. He was afraid that Ellen might turn up and find no one waiting for her at home.

That must have been about five-thirty, Dan calculated. It was dark out now. There was an icy autumn wind blowing. Joan had checked in with Howard five minutes before Dan called her at the hospital. Ellen was still missing.

—— 13 ——

Dan bolted off the hospital elevator at the third floor and hurried around the corner to the nurses' station. "I'm looking for Beth Gallagher," he said. "I'm her husband."

The nurse pulled out a metal clipboard and flipped open Beth's chart. "She's in twenty-two at the end of the hall," she said, indicating the direction with her pencil.

"Is she all right?"

"She's got a broken arm and her head's cut pretty bad. But she'll be all right. . . ."

At the far end of the corridor, there were half a dozen molded plastic chairs lined up against the wall. A few were filled with visitors.

"She was very lucky," the nurse was saying. "It could have been a lot worse."

Dan looked down the hall at the visitors' section, trying to spot Joan Rogerson. Looking for a solitary middle-aged woman, his gaze brushed over the one holding a child in her lap.

Ellen spotted him first.

"Daddy!" she shouted, hopping off Joan's lap and running down the hall toward him. She was crying, the tension flooding out of her.

Dan knelt down and swept her up in his arms. "Oh, baby!" He was crying, too. Tears streamed down his face as he held her. She felt so tiny, so fragile to him now, so much smaller than he remembered her. He could feel her little heart beating against his. "Oh, my baby! It's okay, Daddy's here."

"She got home half an hour ago. Your friend—Alexandra is it?—dropped her off." Joan Rogerson was smiling for Ellen's sake, Dan knew, but her wounded eyes betrayed the damage the day had done to her. "She seems fine. She told Howard that they'd been at Playland, at the amusement park."

"Are you all right, honey?" Dan whispered to Ellen, who was clinging to him.

She nodded, unable to speak.

"Was it Alex? Was the lady's name Alex, baby?"

Ellen nodded again and burst into tears.

"She went on a lot of rides. Some of them were scary. That's what you told Grandma, isn't it, Elle?" Joan said, stroking Ellen's hair. "She went in a rowboat and was afraid the lady was going to turn it over. And she went on the big roller coaster, not the baby one. The Dragon Coaster. That's a pretty grown-up ride for a little girl, isn't it? She says she doesn't want to go with the lady again. She asked me to tell you that, Dan. She said, 'Nanny, tell Daddy not to send her for me again.' She said the lady said nasty things about her mommy. Is that right, Ellen?" Joan asked gently.

Ellen buried her head in Dan's collar. "Yes," she whispered. "Please, Daddy, I don't want to go with her again."

"She made Ellen kiss her good-bye," Joan said. Tears sprang to her eyes. She pulled a tissue from her pocket and blew her nose. Then she held her arms out for Ellen. "Go on, Dan," she said. "Beth's in there. Why don't you go in and see her now?"

Dan stopped outside the door to Beth's room for a minute, trying to compose himself. He needn't have bothered. She was so heavily sedated, her eyes so swollen and bruised, she couldn't possibly have noticed the agitation he was trying to conceal or the phony smile he'd put on for her.

Her father was at her bedside. He seemed startled to see Dan, then gave him a cold, hard look.

"Howard," Dan said gently, nodding to him.

Beth stirred at the sound of his voice.

"It's Dan," he said. "Everything's going to be all right." He took her hand. "I love you," he whispered. Her eyes opened briefly as she registered his presence. She tried to smile, winced, then pressed his hand, lightly, almost imperceptibly, before her eyelids fluttered shut again.

— 14 —

It was pouring by the time Dan got back to the city. He parked the rented car on Gansevoort and, pulling his collar up against the rain, ran across the cobblestone street. He huddled under the wooden eaves of the packing plant next door to Alex's building. He didn't have to wait long. A young couple came out of the building and he slipped past them into the hallway before the door closed.

Out of the traffic noises and pelting rain, in the sudden stillness, Dan became aware of his thudding heart, the pulsing of blood in his temples, the buzz of adrenaline in his ears. He took the stairs two at a time. He didn't bother looking on top of the gas meter for the key. He rang the bell, and waited, shifting from foot to foot like a fighter.

A moment later Alex opened the door a crack. She peered out over the short security chain. This time she was not expecting him. Her eyes widened with fear. She tried to slam the door shut.

Dan exploded. He slammed his shoulder against the door with all his force, with the strength of all his pent-up rage. It gave way with a cracking tear of wood as the chain ripped out of the doorjamb.

Alex, barefoot and wearing a white T-shirt dress, was flung backward into the hall. The door's impact knocked her down. She fell hard against the wall as Dan crashed through the door.

The look of savagery on his face sent her skittering desperately along the hallway. Clawing the floor, she tried to crawl away, but Dan threw himself on her.

She escaped. She kicked and twisted and clawed out of his grasp, then got to her feet and raced toward the living room, throwing down whatever she could reach to block him. She knocked a floor lamp down behind her, then her bicycle, which was leaning against the wall.

It didn't slow him down very much. He jumped over the up-ended lamp and over the bike sprawled in his path, following her through the living room's double french doors into the bedroom.

At the far end of the bedroom, the bathroom door with its frosted glass panel was open. Alex slipped through it a moment before Dan reached to grab her. She pulled the door shut, pinning his arm.

Dan yelled out in pain, then grabbed her head and pulled it violently toward him, toward the thick glass panel separating them. Alex's face pressed grotesquely against the glass. She shook her head, struggling to free herself. He reversed gears and pushed the door open, and she fell back with a loud smack onto the white tile floor.

Dan flung himself through the door and lunged for her. He caught her hair, but she twisted her head out of his grasp, hurled herself backward, and kicked out at him. She caught him in the groin. Dan stumbled back, crashing into the towel rack. The pain surprised him, and he winced. By the time he opened his eyes again, Alex was up and out of the bathroom.

He pushed off the wall and went after her. She sprinted to the far end of the bedroom and ran through the french doors, slamming one behind her. Dan crashed into it, sending shards of glass flying everywhere.

The explosive noise surprised Alex. She turned, lost her balance, and slipped on the cascading glass. Dan tackled her. He caught her ankles, flattening her. Her knees and chest hit the floor with a thudding crunch. She wriggled wildly, clawing and thrashing in the splintered glass.

Dan held her. She tossed her head. She glared at him. Crushed glass glittered in her hair and on her face. A thin scratch on her cheek was filling with blood. She saw him staring at her and she smiled.

It unnerved him. He loosened his grip, for a second. She rolled over, out of his grasp. She kicked him, missing his head, catching him in the shoulder. She tried to get to her feet, but slipped again and, on her hands and knees, scrambled across the floor into the kitchen.

Dan caught her. He yanked her up and slammed her head into the kitchen cabinet. She tried to get away, but he spun her around and smashed her against the stove, sending the light above it swinging madly.

His hands gripped her throat. He held her as she thrashed wildly in his grasp. She tore at his fingers. He tightened his grip. She began gulping for air. His fingers pressed against her windpipe. He could feel it under his thumbs, he could snap it.

He stared at Alex as she flailed in his grasp. He watched her gasping and choking. He saw tears beading at the corners of her eyes. He saw the frail scar on her cheek dotted with blood, the glass shining in her hair, and the jagged chip clinging to her forehead.

He saw Alex. And he let her go. He pushed her away and watched without interest as she skittered backward, staring at him. Finally she turned and ran to the sink. Coughing and sputtering, she splashed water on her face.

Dan turned his back on her. He rested his forehead on the cool enamel of the refrigerator door and tried to catch his breath. It was over. The boiling rage was gone. He stood there, panting, leaning against the refrigerator door, stunned at how close he'd come to killing her.

The sound of his own labored breathing began to fill his head. He was tired. It was time to go.

He started out of the kitchen. A shattering scream stopped him. Dan spun around. Alex Forrest was charging at him with a kitchen knife raised high over her head.

His arm shot out instinctively, catching her wrist. Holding her hand, he whirled her against the side of the refrigerator. She would not let go of the knife. He twisted her arm and tried to pry open her fingers. Finally, with all the strength he had left, he forced her hand up and slammed it against the water pipe next to the refrigerator.

The pain made her release her grip. Dan grabbed the knife and backed away from her slowly, while she held on to the counter for support.

Alex watched him. With a strange, sad smile she watched as he backed away, put the knife on the counter next to the stove, and wordlessly turned and walked out.

It wasn't until he was out of her apartment that he noticed the silence again. He realized that there'd been music playing in Alex's loft. He realized, as he started down the stairs, that she'd been listening to *Madame Butterfly*.

"She's crazy! Don't you get it?"

It was early morning. Detective Lieutenant Russo was sipping decaf from a Styrofoam cup.

"And she's dangerous. I told you before, but you didn't want to listen to me! Now she took my child right out of school! It was kidnapping, pure and simple."

Russo set down the cup and held up his hands as if warding off Dan's anger. "I know," he said calmly, ambling from behind his desk to close the open door to the squad room.

"My wife's lying in the hospital. She's lucky to be alive. If you don't do something about this woman, I—"

"Take it easy, okay?" Russo said. "You don't have to shout."

Dan sat back in the chair facing the lieutenant's desk. "All right. What are you going to do?"

Russo returned to his chair. "We'll get New York to pick her up and bring her in for questioning. Okay?"

"Okay," Dan said, mollified. "Now I'm going to pick up my wife from the hospital. And hopefully I'll be at home for the weekend . . . if you need to talk to me." He stood up. "Thank you, Lieutenant."

Russo lifted his cup of decaf. "You're welcome," he said.

Dan helped Beth into the house. Her left arm was in a cast. She moved slowly, with some pain. Ellen ran inside and closed the door on Quincy, who had chased her rambunctiously up the front walk.

"He's too wild," Ellen explained. "He's going to knock Mommy down."

"Upstairs?" Dan asked.

Beth nodded. "I think so. I'd like to rest for a bit." Gently he helped her up the stairs.

"Mom," Ellen called after them. "I'm going

to make you a baloney sandwich, okay? Do you want one?"

"Thanks, honey," Beth said. "But not right now, okay, sweetie?"

"Elle, why don't you feed Quincy. You can let him in the kitchen, okay?"

"Okay," Ellen said. "I'll make Quincy a baloney sandwich."

The painkillers had made Beth drowsy. She fell asleep quickly. Dan sat in the little armchair across from the bed and watched her for a while. Then he got up and walked from room to room on the second floor. He looked down at the backyard from the window in Ellen's room and saw the rabbit pen, with its forlorn-looking open door. He resolved to dismantle it later, after Ellen was asleep, or early tomorrow morning before she woke up.

The sight of the hutch reminded him that there were a couple of things he needed to do. He went downstairs and phoned the Bedford police station.

Russo was out, the desk sergeant told him. He was expected back late afternoon, early evening. "Right," the sergeant said. "Gallagher. I know. I recognized your voice. You feeling a little better, Mr. Gallagher?"

"Whole lot better," Dan said. "Sorry about the shouting."

"Hey, okay by me. And Russo don't rattle easy anyway."

"I noticed."

He hung up and went out to the car and got his briefcase from the backseat. He carried the case up to the bedroom where Beth was dozing. He pulled the gun he'd bought out of the briefcase and quietly slid open the bedside-table drawer.

Beth stirred. "Dan?"

"It's me. Sorry, baby."

"What are you doing?" Beth asked, squinting sleepily at him.

"Just putting something away in the drawer."

"Mmmm," she said. "What?"

He stroked her hair gently. "Tell you later, okay?"

"Okay." She rolled over, turning her back to him. He was on his way out of the room. "Dan," she called, "was it a gun?"

"Yeah."

"Okay."

15

"So are you going to stay, Dad?" Ellen wanted to know as he was getting her ready for bed.

Dan was at the window when she asked. It was pitch black outside. The only light out back was coming from inside the house, casting thin long shadows on the sloping lawn. The wind whistled through the yard, rattling the bushes and sending bare branches creaking and tapping against the house.

Dan pulled the curtain shut. "Yes," he said, walking back to Ellen's bed. He pulled the covers up to her chin and tucked her in. "You all cozy and snuggly, honey? You want your Uni doll?"

"Uh-huh," she said.

Dan slipped the stuffed toy into bed with Ellen. "Anything else, baby?"

"My Sucky."

"What? This faded old dirty old raggedy old thing?" He reached into his sleeve and, with a flourish, pulled out the treasured bit of cloth from her baby blanket.

"Uh-huh." Ellen giggled.

He handed the piece of patchwork cloth to her and she rubbed it against her cheek with a little contented sigh.

"Good night, honey." He leaned over and kissed her.

"Is Mommy going to be all right?"

"Mommy's going to be fine. You go to sleep now, okay? Should I give Uni a kiss good night?"

"Uh-huh."

Dan gave the doll a kiss.

"Are you going to stay with us?"

"Of course I'm going to stay with you. Didn't I say yes? Sure. Now you go to sleep and have nice dreams, okay? And don't let the bedbugs bite. Good night, darling."

"Dad?"

He'd gotten up. "Yes, baby?" he asked from the door.

"Forever? Promise?"

"I promise. Good night."

Dan shut the light and closed the door.

"Leave it open a peek," Ellen said.

He did.

Beth was leaning over the tub in her bathrobe. Dan crossed the bedroom and looked in on her. "You okay? Can you manage that?"

"Of course," she said, turning on the faucets. The water thundered out, steaming hot.

"Want me to adjust it?"

"I'm okay."

"Okay, good," he said, and went back into the bedroom and snapped on the TV, then dialed the Bedford police station.

Russo was in. "Bad news," he said. "They can't find her."

"What do you mean?"

"New York called. They sent a couple of guys around to pick her up. She's gone."

"What do you mean gone? Why didn't you call me?"

"I was waiting to hear from them. The New York crew. They've been going by her place every couple of hours. They'll be calling in, another twenty minutes or so."

"Do they have any idea where she might be?"

"No."

"Did they check with her neighbors?"

"I believe they did."

Absentmindedly, Dan slid open the drawer in the bedside table and glanced at the handgun. He slid the drawer shut again.

"Well, thanks," he said. "If you hear any more about it, any more information, please be sure and call me—"

"I'll do better. I'll send a squad car around.

Just to cruise the neighb. Okay? They'll spot-check your area every twenty, thirty minutes or so, till we hear from New York that they've got her. Okay?"

"Thanks, Lieutenant. Good-bye."

Dan hung up the phone. He walked to the window and peered out. Beth's tub had already begun to fog the windows. He rubbed a circle in the steam and looked out at the front walk. The light was on. A couple of dry leaves floated past it. The rest of the world was dark. He pulled the bedroom drapes closed, went to the linen closet in the hall, and picked up a pile of fresh towels for Beth. Then he carried them into the bathroom.

"Here you go," he said. The bathroom was steamed up. Beth turned toward him through the haze.

"Thanks," she said.

"How's the arm?"

She smiled at him. "It hurts."

"I'll get you some more of those painkill-ers, okay?"

"Thanks," she said.

The tub water was still running when Dan returned. Beth was inspecting her bruised eye in the mirror. She was startled when he walked in.

"Sorry," Dan said gently. He handed her the pills. "Holler if you need anything else."

Beth smiled at him. "Thanks. I'd love a cup of tea," she said.

"You got it."

Downstairs, he double-locked the front door and put on the security chain. Quincy followed him from the front hall into the kitchen. Dan filled the teakettle with water and set it on the stove. While it heated, he turned the key in the back-door lock and bolted the door, top and bottom.

He walked back to the foot of the stairs. He could hear the TV droning in the bedroom and the tub water still running. It made him nervous. It had been running for quite a while. "Beth?" he called. "Are you in the bathroom?"

He heard the faucet squeak as she turned it and lowered the water to a steady trickle. Then she shuffled out into the upstairs hallway. "Yes?"

"I'm sorry, honey. I just wanted to know if you were okay?"

"I'm okay," she said.

She smiled at him. She'd pinned her hair up. He could see bruises on her neck.

She must have noticed him looking. She pulled up the collar of her white terry robe and tried awkwardly to tighten the belt.

She looked terribly vulnerable, he thought, with her black eyes and puffy mouth. He felt a great rush of love for her, and then a wave of unbearable sorrow for the pain he'd caused. "Beth?"

"Yes?" she said.

He thought of Alex.

"Nothing." He tried to smile at her. "The tea's almost ready. I'll be right up."

Beth returned to the bathroom and tested the water in the tub, leaving the slow stream of hot water running as the level rose to the top. She stepped over to the mirror through the billowing steam, putting a hand cautiously to one eye and pressing gently. It didn't hurt much, but it was hideous. Beth strained to see herself in the foggy mirror, then reached for a towel and wiped a small spot.

Her heart stopped. A figure was coming toward her, materializing out of the steam. It was Alex. Beth whirled around and knocked a bottle off the sink.

Downstairs, Dan was squatting in front of the fireplace, so lost in thought that he didn't hear the faint breaking of glass. He was exhausted. His time away from Beth and Ellen had been painful, and he hoped the reconciliation would bring them all back to normal. Dan shut his eyes. Normal. After all that had happened, his life would never be normal again. He knew it was only a matter of time before the police found Alex, but until then he wasn't safe.

* * *

"What are you doing here? Why are you here? This is where *I* belong. With him."

Alex's voice was low and dull, but she spoke with genuine concern. Beth stared back at her, frozen, unable to utter a sound. Where was Dan? How could this crazy woman have come in without him knowing? A dull glint caught her eye, and her heart leapt again. Alex was holding a knife. She raised it, holding it poised inches from Beth's stomach. Helpless, Beth could only watch in horrified fascination as Alex continued talking in a soft monotone.

"He tried to say goodbye to me. Last night. But he couldn't. You see, Beth, we both feel the same way. You know how it is sometimes, when two people meet for the first time—that instant attraction? When you just *know*? Like a . . . an explosion? That's how it was with us."

The water had finally reached the rim of the tub and started pouring over the side. It spread across the floor around both women's feet, rolling into the bedroom.

And Alex kept talking. Beth was completely mesmerized by the calmness of her voice and the intensity in her eyes. A slight ripping sound made her break her gaze, and she looked down in horror at the knife. It was no longer pointed at her. Alex was mechanically slashing at her own leg, slicing into her thigh and staining her white dress with blood. She slashed again and her voice suddenly got bitter.

"God, how did it all get so fucked up? I don't blame Dan. He told me about you, he was always totally honest. We just couldn't . . . help ourselves. We filled a need in each other's lives. If only you could understand. You'd see how selfish you were being."

Her expression became more menacing as she cut herself deeper and faster. "Do you think I don't know what you were trying to do?" she asked accusingly. "Moving him out to the country, shutting him away, playing happy family. Trying to get him all to yourself! Emotional blackmail. You can't keep a man that way." Her voice continued to rise. "Selfish. You're a selfish stupid bitch. If you knew the unhappiness you've caused. But it can't go on like this. I won't let it."

Dan went back into the kitchen. The teakettle hadn't begun to whistle yet. One of Ellen's fruit rollups was on the table. He picked it up and carried it over to the trash, then changed his mind and ate it.

There was a scratching at the back door. Quincy stirred. "It's the wind, boy," Dan said. It had carried a twig up from the lawn and tossed it against the door, a twig or a stray piece of wood from the rabbit hutch.

He thought of Alex.

The telephone mounted near the back door caught his eye. He looked at it, half expecting it to ring, and suddenly the hair on the back of his neck bristled.

He heard a noise upstairs. Footsteps in the bathroom, creaking overhead. It might have been Beth, but he thought of Alex.

He could feel her presence in the house.

Quincy looked up at the ceiling. Dan followed his gaze. But the teakettle distracted him, shrieking wildly, and he nearly jumped out of his skin. He laughed at himself and hurried to the stove.

Quincy looked up again and whimpered. Dan followed the dog's gaze. He looked up at the ceiling. Water was dripping down.

He lifted the kettle off the heat. But the shrieking didn't stop.

Alex laughed at Beth, swinging wildly with the knife. For a moment Beth didn't think she would be able to move. But she raised her arm to block the plunging knife and smashed Alex in the face with her cast. Alex reeled back and fell against the tub as the knife fell from her hand and skidded across the smooth tile to the corner.

"Dan!" Beth screamed, finally freeing her voice.

Dan bolted up the stairs. Water was flooding from the bedroom now, and each pounding footstep made a small splash on the carpet.

Alex grabbed Beth's ankle and pulled, bringing her crashing to the wet floor. As Beth struggled to get away, Alex retrieved the knife and brought it down hard at her, barely missing.

Dan burst into the bathroom and slammed violently into Alex, smacking her into the medicine cabinet. The glass shattered into hundreds of shards around them.

Ellen was standing at the bathroom door. "Mom! Mom!" she shrieked. Beth twisted around and called back, "Ellen, get out of here! Run!"

Suddenly Alex was slashing at Dan, cutting through his shirt and slicing his chest.

"Run, Beth!" He shouted without taking his eyes off Alex. She slashed his forearm, backing him against the edge of the tub. She raised the knife again and Dan stumbled backward. He grabbed the shower curtain for support and fell back, slapping into the back wall of the tub, thudding into the water.

He let go of the curtain just as Alex's knife pierced it at the top and ripped downward, splitting the curtain in half, missing him by inches.

Dan hoisted himself out of the tub and hurled himself toward Alex. He tackled her and whirled ferociously, slamming her head into a wall with such force that he heard the tiles crunch. Her arm flew back and upended a shelf of cosmetics, sending them flying across the room.

As Dan forced her back against the bath-tub, her knife slashed viciously though she could not see. He had his forearm under her chin and was forcing her head back over the edge of the tub, but her arm continued to flail. Her hand clung to the knife, and she slashed wildly at Dan though her head was underwater now.

Dan lifted her suddenly and flipped her into the tub. Then he dove in on top of her, seizing her throat with both hands. He squeezed her throat, and held her head underwater. Blood from the cuts on his forearm and chest red-dened the water in which Alex flailed. She was struggling against him. Slashing impotently. Twisting ferociously to escape his death grip.

Slowly the struggle was going out of her, but she continued to kick and twist herself underwater. Dan could feel her weakening, so he loosened his grip on her throat. With a last burst of adrenalin, Alex twisted to the side and nearly raised her head above the surface, but Dan pressed down on her again and pinned her to the bottom of the tub. His breathing was loud and heavy, and he could only think about ending the struggle.

It seemed like an eternity before Alex was finally still. Her body was completely limp. A final trail of bubbles drifted up from her mouth, then the water was still. Only then could Dan take his hands from her neck. He gazed down at her and shuddered, then turned away. He lowered himself to the edge of the tub and sat, gasping for breath. He had killed her. It was beginning to sink in now. He'd had to stop her. Now she was dead.

The sudden rush of water was deafening. Dan glanced over his shoulder just as Alex rose above the surface. She had never lost her grip on the knife, and now it was plunging forward, straight at Dan. His muscles locked in terror, waiting for the searing heat of the knife tearing through his flesh.

A shot rang out. Alex was stopped with her arm in the air and hurled back into the tub. The blood poured from the hole in her chest and mushroomed in the water.

Beth stood in the doorway, the gun in her hand. Her arm hung limply by her side, and suddenly the gun looked large and awkward in her grip. Her face was stained with tears; she began to shake violently. Dan stood and moved to her, taking her in his arms. They stood together in the silence of the room, punctuated by Beth's intermittent sobbing. The words she'd spoken to Alex on the phone rang in Dan's mind. *If you ever come near my family again, I'll kill you.*

"It's over," he whispered, still holding Beth tightly.

The nightmare was over, but the scars would never heal.

THE LAUGHTER AND THE TEARS

**Buy them at your local
bookstore or use coupon
on next page for ordering.**